GW00836261

The Wrenna

R. M. Francis

Wild Pressed Books

The Wrenna © 2021 by R. M. Francis.

Contact the author via twitter: @RMFrancis

Editor: Tracey Scott-Townsend

Cover Design by Tracey Scott-Townsend

ISBN: 978-1-9163774-3-1

Published by Wild Pressed Books: 2021

http://www.wildpressedbooks.com

To Ernest, Stanley, David and Paul. Men of
graceful strength.

The Wrenna

There you'll find the place I love most in the world. The place where I grew thin from dreaming.

   – Juan Rulfo

The Ley

It's the Wren's Nest – part housing estate, part nature reserve – it's the Wrenna to us. Frogspawn slicks in silica sheets across Green Pool; carrion crow calls; the foxes den – too close to the road – vixens crushed against tarmac; limestone cliffs weathered by prehistoric waves; the underground caves – the fenced off caverns – the canal lines that vein through; rabbits, badgers, weasels; and rusted cans and cigarette buts and flytipped sacks and discarded clothes and the stained knickers of a fallen wench; limes, acorn, hawthorn, bluebell and stinky wild garlic; bell pits, old mine shafts and geological tools; dog walkers amble through slippery tributaries of homemade paths; rope-swinging kids up a height in the oaks; the silence; the almost-silence; the rhizomes that pierce through earth's hymen and tangle, conjugate.

None of this is metonym. This land is where we live. The Wrenna. Here is where they dug into the earth and pulled out a giant trilobite – the Dudley Bug, they call it – not a metonym. The streets orbit the woods – not as a symbol, literally. Terraces; clad in cobblestone and redbrick, meander, side stream, feed, branch, in swirls around the pull of the woods. The estate eddies the woods.

Grandson lives with his brood three streets down from Nan who took the cousin's house who now lives up by our auntie, she's been there for three generations and the kids'll have it after too, and John and Wendy are two doors up from her sister and their babs are just through the alley next to our kid who used to live with her best friend at school and she's only a stone's throw from her grandson. Every bloodline webs our Wrenna like this.

You say don't walk through here at night. You say to be careful. Avoid us. But we are here. Like the frogspawn sticking to the film of algae, we are cells, sucking at light, stunned in our own kind of beauty.

Shavers End Reservoir One

I tried to jump the pale stone wall. I couldn't make it in one leap anymore. I took three breaths on its top before easing myself down. Blood from my hands stained the cold stone. The mist stroked the concrete and steel of the reservoir's bulwark. I stepped up, tip tapping soles against metal steps. I stared at the blood staining my hands and clothes. I stared at the dark waters. Stared like I'd done every time I'd been caught, almost been caught, wanted to be caught. My reflection stared back at me from the water – neatly shaved hair, stubbled face, my pale sunken eyes. I was caught in the stare. Blood. Mist. Water. Stillness. And a hessian sack gripped in my fist. I opened it.

Them gangs am gonna want me to mek amends, pay fer it. Them gonna want absolution or abolishment. Mom'd say, mek em wait an' they wo' do nothin', mek 'em wait an' remember what yower old mon tode yo'.

Foxglove Road

In the springtime, the moon still thinks it's night when we walk to school.

"Juno 'utton, get yower arse in this 'ouse at once," called Mother Hutton. Her yawp echoed out through the criss-cross streets, bounced off the pebbledash terraces and into the woods, all through the underground caves that make up The Wrenna.

She stood at the bottom of the street, hands on hips. Calling out across the Wren's Nest Road, up over the bonk and into the trees.

"Yo'll starve than 'ave a charred tay, Juno 'utton. It'll gu to the wammel if yo' ay back in ten."

We all knew it was time for tea when we heard that call.

I'd been tadpoling down Green Pool when I heard it. The racket made me spill the jar over the grasses. All those black, speckled half-beings wriggling and gasping, jutting and jittering on the grass as their brown water soaked into the earth. I scooped as many up as I could – launched them back into the pond. The birds had started circling before I even made it to the path. That's where she was. Coming the other way, Juno.

The paths are narrow through the woods. I waved to let her go first. My eyes bowed.

"Cheers," she said.

She spoke to me. I didn't look up. It was only a few seconds or maybe she waited for me, I had to catch my breath and I had to stop myself from gasping and my face was cold and the sun blared through the beeches onto my sweating neck. I'm sure she was looking at me. *Say hello. Don't say hello. That's Juno Hutton, you moron. Say something.*

"Thass yower mom, ay it?" I asked.

"It is ar. 'Er gus mad if the tays burnt."

"Juno, ay it?"

"Thass me. Who am yo'?"

Juno was in year ten, I was still a year eight. Everyone knew her. She was the first name everyone learnt at school. She lived in the next street across from me, Foxglove Road. We followed her home sometimes. I looked down at my feet – filthy from the muddy edges of Green Pool. The bottom of my jeans, mud-caked. Even my hands were dirty – laced in slime that had started to get sticky in the sun.

"Who am yo' then?" she asked again. She studied me. She tried to get the measure of my eyes that sat slightly too far back in their sockets and were framed with dark rings.

I raised my head from my hands. But only as far as her tits. They were huge. Huge, round, fleshy mounds

8

packed into her school blouse, her tie dropping gently between them. She'd had tits since Wrens Nest Primary, but now . . . Jesus.

"Dirty little shit," she said and strutted off.

I went hot and cold and hot and shivery and wanted to laugh and cry and fall over and throw a stone at her and try and catch her up and tell her my name and maybe we'd get to like each other, and she might fancy a younger guy like me, and I was hungry and my stomach was in knots and I sweated and maybe she might want to come to mine for tea sometime and maybe . . . I don't know.

As she strode out down the path towards the houses she dropped something. A fist of flowers. Pink bells. I picked them out of the hawthorn. I still have those flowers from the woods. I pressed the pink petals in a copy of the Ladybird Book of Custer's Last Stand. I picked them out of the hawthorn. I got a graze or a splinter or sting or something. I sucked at it. Forgot about the tadpole mucus slicked over my hands.

"Dirty little shit," I whispered. I smiled. I gave my fingers another taste.

Woodsorrel Road

Our lot were all at Bishop's Milner school, so we had no choice really, we had to go. Still, the Pentecost fete was pretty cool. We had to sing loads of psalms and the babs from the primary school had their first communion in the morning, but after that they had rides and music and they roasted a pig.

"How many pieces, bab?" Nan asked.

"One please, Nan."

Nan never missed these things. She played organ in the church sometimes. And sometimes Father Stephen let her sing an old Welsh Hymn. *Ni chaiff dim amharu'th gyntun. Ni wna undyn â thi gam.* When Mom married Dad she moved from Woodsorrel Road to Old Park Road. Nan was happy about that. Most families are like that round here. None of us move far. Nan didn't like how they opened their shop on a Sunday, especially at Whitsun. But she didn't judge.

I scoffed the hot pork cob down and ran off to the Astroturf. I was always alright upfront. I scored three with my head – I normally did, I was taller than the rest and no one was a goalkeeper except for Burroughs and he was a prick. He was one of those man-child sorts who started shaving when they were eleven and had shoulders like most of the dads, he played for Stourbridge Town now. He had funny eyes, like he was tired and angry and sad and scared. Everyone knew Burroughs. He was the second name you learned at school. Most people at least knew someone who'd taken grief from him. When Alvan moved to the Wrenna, Burroughs spent the first three weeks robbing his dinner money. Me and Nick put a stop to that.

All the parents were canting and eating cake and the rides were playing that jingle-jangle music and the younguns were doing cartwheels and pretending to be Ironman or Captain America and the older kids were being weird or hard or unseen and we were shouting *One-two! Cross! Hand ball!* A group of six or seven men stood, looking in, whispering in a strange language by the gates. Looking back, that's how it started. Just a few. Then a few more. Then the gangs.

Then I saw her. Well, I heard her. Over by Nan and Father Stephen was this girl. More than a girl. I'd seen her about but not *seen-seen* her before. Pale. Small. Brown bobbed hair. Brown eyes. She stood in front of the grown-ups, hands behind her back. Her summer dress all white and creased. I noticed that. The creases. What girl was this? I heard her. We all did. We stopped.

"Guide me o thou great redeemer!"

She sang softly and slowly and she made me think of winter. I walked over to Nan.

"Bread of Heaven, Bread of Heaven, feed me til I want

no more!"

I was out of breath from the footie and the pork had made me sick in my mouth. Stunned and hot and cramped and dizzy. I stood next to Nan and watched her. Her eyes met mine and she looked down and I looked away and I think we both half-smiled. Nan joined in the second verse.

"Agor y ffynhonnau melus."

Two tongues tempering the Pentecost fete.

With my eyes I traced the outline of the girl's arm, waist, legs, down to two tiny feet – white socked in filthy shoes. Filthy shoes. *What girl is this?* Stomach empty, gums leaking. Sweet-bitter saliva seeping around my cheeks. I couldn't help but smile. She was snow-skinned with wide, wild eyes – deep brown. Dark hair, matted and windswept. *What girl is this?* I stood stunned.

We all clapped when she stopped.

"What a beautiful song," Father Stephen said. "And an even more beautiful voice, Olwen."

Olwen! *What girl is this?* I didn't want to look up again. Nan placed her bony fingers on my shoulder and pinched. I'd never seen her smile so wide.

Little by little the sounds started up around me again. Football shouts, grown-up chatter, the clink-clank of rides and the jangle of coins. I looked at Olwen and then away and then at Nan and I wanted to go home and I wanted to say something and maybe I'd show her Green Pool and where the newts and frogs had started to spawn but not that, no, maybe we could

12

go to the baths or something and I had to leave soon and I heard a goal scored at the other end so they might need me back. I felt sick and full and sort of sleepy – that sharp cuckoo bread taste – and I felt that feeling like you should probably sit down to hide it. The twinge. The growth. And she sort of smiled. I'm sure she did.

"Live for beer! Live for beer! Drink and Drink until you drop!" Burroughs had started singing a few feet away.

I went red immediately. The sickness left me. The twinge. The oddness. I was clear, raged. I couldn't help myself. I turned away from Nan and Olwen. Took three strides and hit him. I hit him like Dad showed me – two fists into the body, one on the belly and one on the V of his ribs. He choked. Fell back. Hit the deck. I don't even know if I knew properly, but there was something needed kicking back against there. Olwen, beauty, the people around – it needed defense.

All those years later, I'd been away and returned, I started collecting cuttings from the Dudley News, kept them under my bed with my Navy stuff – headlines about girls going missing, and fights between opposing gangs, and the bill they'd got through the Commons and into the Lords about reducing sentences. It was only a few at first, just a handful from the first tranche that'd been released, but they sort of called out to others when they were released, and it soon built. Mates on the inside became toops on the outside. I'd get these cuttings out from under my bed, and I'd look

13

at them and look through my Navy stuff and felt that redness, that sickness, that twinge. I was clear. I was raged.

Within seconds Nan had slapped me around the back of the head. Her bony fingers clipped the top of my ear. She marched me back to Woodsorrel Road.

"You're not singing anymore!" Someone sang from the crowd.

Sometimes I still see the look on Olwen's face as Nan led me away. Those wide eyes squinted. Her brow furrowed. Eyebrows curled. Pink lips pursed. It's blurred. I can't see if it's a smirk or a frown. I still taste that Cuckoo Bread sharpness, too.

Harebell Crescent

It was the first time in ten years the photo album had been out. I was hiding in the loft amongst the dust and dark, the flotsom and jetsom of our marriage. I punched the roofbeam. My knuckles were used to it now. Looking at the photos I saw her leaving again and again – the breeze flicking and ticking at the blue raincoat she always wore. Blue was her colour. Blue through and through. I threw the photos across the loft.

I'll get her back or I'll get back at her.

I punched the roofbeam again. The bloodstain stamped from my knuckle made a pact against the wood.

There's a house on Harebell Crescent that no one goes near. Well, the kids chuck bibbles at the windows from time to time and there was that odd time on Halloween when we were twelve and everyone had a story about Thirteen Harebell Crescent but other than that no one goes near it.

It's boarded up now. I couldn't say if it's council and they can't be arsed or maybe that man bought it when

Thatcher gave us the green light. He's dead now. No one's home.

All the houses on the Wrenna, well most of them, are sort of dirty-cream-coloured with pebbledash and the woodpanes are normally cracked and damp. Sometimes there's car parts and old sofas and the black pitch left from bonfires, rusty washing machines. But you know, they looked after the gardens. They all had well-kept flower beds with tall Glads and Roses and those grasses with the orange flowers.

She finished her shift at 6am. The workers left through the back and she was the same. They all walked around the nature reserve. She cut through it. That's where I used to meet her with the dog each morning. That's where I met her that morning. I left the dog at home. I took the leash with me.

Thirteen Harebell Crescent was boarded up with plywood and spray-canned with names and curses. *Juno Hutton is a slag. EDL. Batty Boy Burroughs.* Once I saw someone had put *This is Art* on the terrace end. Most are boarded up now. A lot of people moved out when some of the girls started disappearing. The patrolling gangs use it to cut through. We stay on our own streets now.

If you got around the back and scrambled through the goosegrass and bramble you could see how some of us had prized the wood away from the little window that led to the basement.

The front yard was a small cube overgrown with grass, nettles and flocks of delicate, purple flowers.

Their convex caused the colour to flex in different shades. Breezes made them shiver. They made their way through all the thick green and brown weeds – spotting the whole yard right up to the front step, the lounge window, the cracked path. Purple spotted shivers against the weathered and the wild.

No one goes near thirteen Harebell Crescent.

That fucking Sheila nextdoor. Fucking phoned the police, day 'er? I was keeping Karin in the basement. I fed her and give her a bath and let her walk about, and she had water and free room down there. I had to lamp her the first couple of times but she soon understood.

"We've had reports of strange noises," the officer said.

"My boiler's playin' up but I'm behind with the council and them being blether 'eads about it."

They asked a few other questions and had a little snoop and they asked about Karin and I said she was with her mom.

That's when it started. I ay a queer. I knew Sheila'd keep watch and er'd be cantin' down the coffee mornings. I started prancing up and down the road with her blue raincoat on. Got myself a wig. Made sure she was seen.

When we crept in that one Halloween we saw stuff.

We jumped the back fence and gave legs-up to the smaller lads. Climbed through the thicket of back garden and started kicking and pulling at the boards.

"I'm in!" Nick said. "I'm fuckin' in 'eya!"

Nick gave it one last boot and then started pulling at the thick splinter he'd cast into the plywood.

"Weem in."

Like I say this window went to the basement. One of them high in the corner, narrow windows. We were kids but even we had to breathe in to pinch through. Hands and arms first. Then head – turned sideways. A quick breast-stroke kick and the shoulders, chest, and belly follow. That's when you feel it – the need to gasp, to blow out, to squirm. That tadpole left on the field feeling. And you might wriggle a bit, and you might panic, but you catch your bone or flesh on the jagged windowpane and that brings you back. Then it's slide inward, downward into the basement.

"Fuckin' hell, whass that smell?" I called back. I was first down. "Smells like Juno's snatch."

"Smells like your mom's snatch," Nick said.

They all laughed, I had to give him that one, so I laughed too.

It stank of old paint, damp soil, vinegar. Like Green Pool when it gets too hot. Like the yeast from the bakers and fat at the back of Bennett's Butchers. Rank.

Nick soon followed and we got the others to lay their bikes down by the window and shine the lights in.

There were paint tins and tools and piles of dusty, damp boxes. Bin liners full of rags, old clothes, towels. We rummaged. Tiptoeing, taking tiny breaths. Held up soiled pants with choking laughs. Nick had brought a crowbar and a sledgehammer with him. We threw paint, wood, nails and tools up to the others.

"We'll mek a den wi' these."

If you cor believe it yourself then there ay no one

18

gonna believe it. So, you write and re-write. Rehearse. Rework. I practiced her walk. The way 'er twitched 'er shoulder to 'oist 'er 'andbag. The flick of 'er 'ead to stop 'er fringe gerrin' in 'er eyes. I practiced. We were together for ten years before 'er tried to leave me – love notices all the little things. Love is wide eyed and sniper aware.

"Come eya, mate," Nick said. He was in the corner, arched over a set of drawers. I skipped to him.

"What is it?"

"Bloody perv, ay 'e?"

Nick held out a handful of photographs. Pictures of a bloke taking pictures of himself in the mirror.

"E's a fuckin' tranny!"

And he was. All dressed and dolled up. One of them skinny, short men who always have a menacing look. Years later we knew him as Little Phil. We'd see him getting mulled in The Britannia. Always had a way about him like he wor sure if he wanted to fuck you or fight you. That's what he was like. Short and skinny with sniper eyes. And in the pictures he was in a dress with make-up and trying out different poses. And in some pictures he just had girl's pants on. And in some pictures he'd tucked his goods up between his legs. And sometimes he looked funny and sometimes surprised and sometimes he looked like he'd kill someone.

I put the photos in my pocket.

Then froze.

We heard the tip-tap and clipping of footsteps from

upstairs. *No one lives here.* We froze. The footsteps paced back and forth on the wooden floor. Angry steps. Like Mrs Simpson down the corridors at school.

Me and Nick nodded at each other, and we pulled out.

I gave him a leggy and he pulled my arms from the top. We tossed the bikes over, jumped the gate and legged it home.

'Er lost herself down there and I suppose I did too. I ay sure which of us was fust to go. But I ended it. I ended her.

I stared at those pictures all night. Little Phil. Every detail. Where he'd shaved himself. Where he'd forgot to. His attempt after attempt to perfect. The half-hex of his gaze as he failed. I flicked through photo after photo, alone in the almost dark of my room. And I could almost hear him talk to me. I could almost hear his voice in my head and see his thoughts in my mind and I felt that years later when I'd read about the latest crimes in the Dudley News. He looked back. Watching me watching him fail.

Karin was never found.

Gorse Road

Every now and then I'll get some liver from the butcher. Try that meat jelly, metal-flesh, aspic snap again. I can't figure it out fully. There's something that draws me in. Like how we enjoy our own smells, sometimes. Enjoy being fetid.

Bernadette Carlin looked after us on dark nights, sometimes. There were seven or eight of us. Auntie Carlin, that's what the moms made us call her. They'd go up The Spills Meadow for dominoes. The loser'd have to look after her on a Sunday. Dad said she was his childminder when they were kids, too.

We loved it and we hated it at Aunty Carlin's up on Gorse Road. There was so much clutter – too much. One thing bled into the next. There was no start or end to any of it. Novelty teapots pushed into every inch of shelf space. Archives of old magazines, old 'oss brasses tacked to her fireplace, wall racks of pipes – corncob, clay, meerschaum – framed the hall, stairwell and landing. Plates nailed to plaster, marking every royal event. Bowls of sticky suck. Too much to see. Always open-ended.

She must be dead now.

"See yo' Sundee, Bernie," Mom or Dad'd say. That's when you knew you'd be back in two nights' time.

She'd make liver and onion and we'd do her tops or weed the garden or make sure she wor behind on her bills. She'd always make liver and onion. We'd always have a job.

"Doh 'er know the war's over?" Dad laughed. "'Er doh 'ave to ration an' ate the giblets an' gizzards 'a stuff these days."

"Tek 'er to Nando's, Dad."

"'Er'd 'ave 'eartattack."

Some of the dads on The Wrenna worked with steel and car parts and went scrapping. The liver tasted like they stank. It gave me that back of the mouth top of the nostril feelin'. Like you might sneeze and you might be sick and you might like it too. One day I'd give Nick's Dad's arm a lick – just a quick lap of the sweat and the oil and the steel. Liver.

I'm sure she's dead now. She only ever looked after us on those winter nights.

"Yo' doh see 'er when iss hot."

The only time you saw her when it was getting warmer was on one of those bright winter days that come February half-term. You'd sometimes catch her collecting branches in the woods.

I saw Olwen coming out of there quite a bit. She always looked a bit creased round the edges. Lovely though. One day she came out with a big stick in her hand.

"Here," she said, and prodded me with it. Not hard. Just playful like. But the end of it was freezing. Freezing. I mean, Jack Frost cold. Made me jump out my flesh.

———————

"See this?" Dad said one Sunday. He held up a box of corn dollies. A shoe box filled with writhing and interlocking straw limbs.

"On the fust day 'a Spring every year, yower Auntie Carlin sticks all of these out in the garden, 'er does."

I screwed my face up.

"Iss true. An' on the fust day 'a Autumn, 'er brings 'em all back in."

"Why?"

"Summat about the seasons. Harvest Festival. The moon. Summat like that."

I thought of that when they put the Wicker Man on at Christmas.

———————

Liver made the back of your teeth hurt. Metallic. Pissy. I relived it years later when we did shrooms up on Poplar Crescent. Cold copper absorbed in the muck of grasslands. Earthy. Makes you spit.

"One Sunday," Nick told us weeks after. "'Er 'ad me an' our kid doin' 'er tools."

"Ya wha'?"

"'Er come in the front room," Nick said. "Me an' Paul on 'er rug. An' 'er was 'oldin' a big case of tools. 'Er put 'em down an' 'ad us clean 'em."

"So what?"

"What wench of Bernie's age 'as tools? What wench in 'er nineties needs 'em cleanin? So I ask 'er, an' 'er says: Who'dya think shapes the limestone cliffs an' the caverns on the Wrenna? Thass all 'er said."

How can liver be grainy and squishy at the same time? I still get it from the butchers when the mood takes me. I still can't figure out the metal and the muck. The flesh and the steel.

"Seems right to me," Polish Pete said once. "Liver. Flesh-metal, in Dudley. Seems right." He had a point.

She must be dead now. We don't get much snow anymore.

Dudley Chronicle

A watershed reform of UK justice laws could allow hundreds of prisoners to be released early.

Dudley North Councillor, John Berresford, has spent the last four years campaigning for the rights of those imprisoned who, according to his Think Tank's definition, have been subject to systematic mistreatment by the establishment. He told Dudley News: "A huge proportion of our prison's population are made up of people who have been underrepresented by the political and educational institutions of this country, and have lived lives under great stresses because of this lack and due to their socio-economic situation. This new law recognises the unfairness of this and will strip years off their sentences to help repair the damage."

Berresford's Bill is being debated in the House of Commons this week, and is expected to be passed to the House of Lords by Easter.

Keep up to date with the latest in your community with Dudley News.

Spinney

The upturned seabed that valleys the woods, homes lichen and moss and odd berries. Heart notes of wild garlic. These are cut throughs where nature has rewilded old pits. Top notes of damp soil. Sometimes you'd see a small pile of beige limestone. Like a burial mound. And sometimes the mounds seemed to move. And sometimes you wouldn't see them at all. Base notes of dead insects. I'm not sure how well we remember these things.

Marigold Crescent

Polish Pete lived up Marigold Crescent and he said Sauerkraut makes everything taste better.

"Sauerkraut make everything better," he'd say. "Everything better. Everything."

It was odd really, a man his age and us kids. He day do nothing to us though.

Dad'd tell us "doh gu up that Dudzedski's 'ouse, 'e ay no good, 'e's got them Ukranian Gypsy curses an' all that."

He was a big bloke, Pete. Dead tall. Uneasy on his feet – that tall. He only ever wore tracksuits and always had a bumbag tied around his waist. A bumbag. He was always fidgeting with it, but I never saw him get a thing out. He told us he thought boxing class was a good idea, we'd never know when it might come in, his great-grandad had to fight off the gangs when they started up in Kalisz.

"He was a strong man," Pete said. "They try to obliterate. Always watch out. Look at these gangs from the prisons starting up around here," he said.

When I moved back to the Wrenna it was Pete who first pointed it out to me. He'd said that our estate was cut off and that no one really gave a fuck about what happened over here, and that made it easy for them to set up foundations, and the woods made good cover for taking girls off, and this new joker on the council was obsessed with offering absolution or something and he'd pushed through this bill. It meant that what the prisoners had missed out on because of bad schooling, and lack of opportunities, would be removed from the time they had left to serve of their sentence. And he told us to keep a keen eye on all of that.

He got us drink when we was in year ten. He was fucking Juno then. She'd be at his place too when we came calling. I still had those flowers from the woods. I'd pressed the pink petals in a copy of the Ladybird Book of Custer's Last Stand.

We went to The Priory Boxing Club on Fridays and stayed out at the park after. Dad used to train with a bloke who'd been a Shaolin Monk and he'd shown me a few tricks. I was tall and I had a reach on me too but I knew you should run before you fight and fight before you maim and maim before you kill.

After boxing it'd be whoever was last to get their gloves unlaced to go to Polish Pete's. He'd head down the Priory shops and get us Vodka. It was my turn.

Juno answered to me. I just stood staring. *Fuck.*

"Pete ay in," she said staring at me, smoking. She was nineteen now. She was still a name round here. The same happened again. Those tits. Those beautiful, fleshy, perfectly round, bulging, source of all goodness, pushed in your face, framed by a tight vest top, good lord, tits.

"Yo' again, yo' dirty little shit." She studied me again. Seemed to be tracing the dark rings around my eyes. Tried to figure it out.

I snapped out of it. I wor a virgin no more.

"Pete in?"

"Is back in Poland."

"Oh . . . shit. Soz, Juno, 'ave a good night."

I turned to walk away. Wondered if I was tall enough to try the shop myself now? I had to try. The lads'd love me forever if I did.

"Ay yo' the lad who fucked up Burroughs?"

I turned back. "I am ar."

"Nice one. Prick, ay 'e?"

Burroughs'd offered me out a few weeks after I'd knocked him down for Olwen. She never thanked me.

"I've got vodka in 'ere. Pete brews it. Tastes like shit but it gets yo' wankered."

I turned back fully. Went a bit giddy. The boxing had left me thirsty and I was sweaty but cold and my heart beat a bit harder. Just enough to notice it. I was older now. I went in.

"Shit me. Am yo' shittin' me?" Alvan asked.

"I ay."

"We thought yo'd bin modged by Pete or summat?" Nick said.

"I wor."

"We was gonna gu tell yower old mon."

"Glad yo' day."

"Shit me. Juno 'Utton. What was 'er like?"

She was like nothing else. Before. After. Nothing else. I was pinned to the sofa and I was subjugated and it was as tender as Olwen's voice.

I went back a month later. To see Pete. I was still too young really and I couldn't go to the doctor's. Dr Kaur was a wench and she knew Nan and Dad and Mom. Dr Kaur knew fucking everyone. And she was a wench. I couldn't see a wench doctor.

He stood in the doorway – tracksuit, bumbag – towering.

"Czesc, brother!" Pete said. "Come, come." Beckoned me in with sweeping gestures.

"Cheers, Pete."

"Prosze. You want vodka?"

"No ta. I need some help."

He stopped me in the hall. Held his hands out in front like he was stopping traffic. Eyes wide. Shocked. Put his finger to my lips.

"No speak," he said and just stared at me.

He just stood there, peering at me, rocking his head to and fro. Investigating my face.

"Iss a problem ... sort 'a ... down there." I told him.

He took a step back. Shrugged. His face relaxed.

"Nie ma za co. This is no problem, brother," he said. "Tamta?" he asked, pointing at it.

I nodded. He puckered his lips and nodded back. Held out his hand for me to wait. Scurried off to the kitchen for a few seconds and came rushing back with an enormous grin and a large jar held high in his hand.

"Sauerkraut!" he said. "Fix everything. Take these down," he said, motioning to my shorts.

I did. He unscrewed the lid to the jar and fingered out a large chunk of the wet funk cabbage. Screwed it into a ball. Got on his knees. Pressed it against my cock. It twinged. Grew a little.

"Prosze. This is no worry," he said. "We all have some little . . . you know."

We looked at each other for a second longer than normal. His eyebrows raised. Lips curled in the corners. On his knees. Looking up at me. Hand on cock.

He stood. Motioned again. Held his hands out like he was conducting me, like a sculptor might look at his half-finished piece. Then he walked off.

I just stood there. Bottom naked in the hall of his home. *Please let Juno be out. Don't let him be with any of his crazy polak mates who drink like Oliver Reed and Dance to 90s house music and dance like they're on ketamine and can only shout, they can only shout.* "Yo' cor trust people who cor 'old theya tongue," Nan'd said. "An' yo' cor trust Russians."

Juno. She'd called me a dirty little shit. She was cool and strange and she was strong and she stung me but

31

she stung with soft lips and lithe limbs and control – gentle, rocking, control.

Ten minutes later Polish Pete was back. He plucked the sauerkraut from my cock, rolled it up again. He took thumb and forefinger and clawed my chin. Pulled my mouth open and popped the sauerkraut in. Pushed my jaws shut. He held up a finger and looked deep into me. Then made a chewing gesture.

I started to chew. Sweet. Acid. Rot. Slippery and crunchy. Mom's cabbage was almost a juice when we had it on Sundays. It had nothing.

Pete tapped me on the shoulder, maneuvered me around and walked me to the door.

"Do Widzenia," he said and closed the door.

I started up Marigold Crescent. Swallowed the ferment. Coughed a little. Laughed at myself a bit.

Limes Road

I was back in Mom's old house when I started drinking with Mark. I'd been discharged from the Navy and come home. There were more gangs about. Mark'd always have a skinful.

"Fuckin . . . everyone loves 'er," he said. "We all do, doh we. Fuckin'. 'Er's the best 'a the lorrofus, ay 'er? Fust time I sid 'er we was out at the Gifford Arms, fuckin' great pub that, down in Wolves, iss where the bikers drank. Thass where I sid 'er fust."

He stopped. He looked up at Becky behind the bar. Searched the last dreg of his pint glass.

"Giz another . . . erm, just check me change . . . ar, one more 'alf bab, no, no, no I've gorra another quid 'ere. One more pint, me wench an' two fingers 'a whisky."

Then he started again.

"Fuckin' everyone loved 'er. We all did, day we. I went up to 'er, 'er was wearin' these leggins an' a Bauhaus Tshirt an' 'er looked like Debbie 'Arry, 'er did. 'Er did. 'Er did, ar. Now, my old mon tells stories about him an' my mom meeting an' they say how they danced an' 'e did this and 'er did that it an' it was all Sleepless in Seattle bullshit. That ay 'ow it gus. 'Ow it works is this. I stared at 'er from across the pub. Lovely 'er was. Fuckin' lovely. Then a few days later I sid 'er in the tesco with 'er mom an' I was with my mom. An' I dunno 'ow they knew but it was them who suggested it an' it wor half embarrassing an' I ay gorra clue to this day if I'd ever 'ave said anything. Fuck knows. Thass it though, ay it. Everyone loves 'er. We all do, doh we. Fuckin'. 'Er's the best 'a the lorrofus, ay 'er? I love 'er. 'Er's mine."

Mark was one of those guys who drank every day. Sometimes he'd tell you really long stories about the eighties and how everytime Depeche Mode came back to Brum, Dave Gahan gave him a call. And sometimes he'd just keep saying the same thing over and over again. And sometimes he'd do both. He was sound. He drank every day, and he was one of those annoying bastards who'd get up for work at 4am and feel fine. And he'd fix anything. And he'd be the first in line to come and help if you needed something fixing. And he'd be the last person left standing on The Wrenna.

"Yo' ay gorra kip croppin' yower 'air now yo' ay in the Navy," he said to me. "An' when yo' gonna start sleepin' proper. Get rid 'a them bags under yower eyes. What did yo' see out theya?"

I never said. Never told anyone.

"Dya know, mucker, our Jackie, 'er's fierce 'er is, an' 'er's soft too. See when 'er was a young wench 'er old man used to touch 'er – you know – touch 'er down theya. It was only 'im an' 'er. She day 'ave any sisters or brothers an' 'er mom 'ad run off with some bloke up Eve's Hill. One day ... before I met 'er like, I'd 'a tore 'is fuckin' cock off! Anyway, one day 'e comes at 'er tryin' to touch 'er an' stuff an' 'er smacks 'im, 'er does. Bam! Straight in the nose with 'er 'ockey stick. An' 'er runs off, 'er does. 'Er runs to Dudley Town an' 'er dobs on 'im, 'er does. An' 'e gets sent down. An' years later 'er tells me this an' 'er says to me, 'er says – *I'm all 'is got, 'e was screwed by everyone an' I ay excusin' 'im an' I ay lerrin' 'im off or forgivin', but I'll visit, an' I do. I gu up to Featherstone Prison once a month an' say 'ow do to 'im* – Thass our Jackie."

It was too.   Sometimes you'd see her fish-hook someone outside the Britannia for being a prick. But you'd also see her running the coffee mornings at the community centre for MacMillan Nurses. She put an old tv set through the window of Welsh John's van once cause he owed Mark a week's wage. She took all the kids on Limes Road to see Santa at Dudley Castle every year.

"Yo' watch me an' I'll watch yo'," she said to me once. "An' that works all ways, always."

I thought about all of this when I was going through the stuff under my bed. I thought about it that night up on the reservoir when I was clear and I was raged.

Mrytle Road

We must've been about twelve or thirteen I reckon. Old enough to know. Too young to think it through. It was Alvan who talked us into it. Funny little half-caste kid, he was. His mom was Syrian and his dad was dead. His dad was one of the first to get killed around here – the gangs didn't like men who let their women out acting like she did. In the summer she'd wear the same kind of dresses as Juno Hutton, and I'd seen her share a can of cider with Mom too. Whenever we went up to call for Alvan his mom'd give us Baklava and Cigar nut pies. We'd be up all night. Alvan was always saggy eyed and always wired and he was always late, so we had to sit with his mom while he was getting ready.

"It's too sweet for Dudley tongues, isn't it?" she'd say. "Have some more."

We nodded. She was always feeding us. She always said I needed more fat on my bones. She looked at us for too long sometimes. Her eyes were too dark. You couldn't tell if she was too old or too young to be Alvan's mom. She looked like she'd either just finished crying or was about to start. Nan always said hello, so did the moms. But they day take her to the pub or anything. She always made tons of food for Harvest Festival and the dads used to tease her about how much chilli she could take.

"Ah woulnt mind gerrin' me onds on yower spice rack," they'd say.

"If you could kiss one girl round here who would it be?" Alvan asked us one night.

"Juno Hutton," we answered. That was years before we started going to Polish Pete's.

"My mom said she's a masasa." He'd taught us a few bits of Arabic.

"Who cares?" Nick said. "I'd do 'er."

"Yo'd do what?" I said.

"Do 'er," Nick said. "Do 'er." Nick was wide eyed and pullin at his cock.

"You don't know what IT is." Alvan said.

Alvan 'ad is dad's eyes, so he said. He was odd. Tanned skin and bright blue eyes.

There was one summer me and our Nick went up Myrtle Road every day to play with him. We'd break branches off the trees in the woods and carry them back to Alvan's. Strap them together with string and shoelaces and tape. We had stuff we'd stolen from the haunted house on Harebell Crescent. His mom'd given us her old abayas to make walls.

"This all they good for now. You rip them, dirty them, do what you want, my boys."

"Thanks, Mrs Maleh."

"Afwan, my boys. Ahlan wa sahlan."

"Wass 'er talkin' that paki language for?" Nick said. Alvan kicked 'im in the shin. They both laughed.

I reckon it took us about three days. I was skinny, but strong. Still am. We'd lashed the wood together. Wrapped Mrs Maleh's old robes around it. Covered the roof in wood and corrugated iron we'd nicked from the back of Mr Patel's. "It's a Sukkah," Alvan said. "Our Sukkah."

"A fuckin' what?" Nick said. "A sucker? Like a dick sucker."

"Suk-Kah!"

"Oh, Suk-k-k-kah! Alright, fuckin' rag 'ead."

"Learn to speak, snow white."

"Snow white? Is that all you've got, Isis?"

"Alright. Fucking. Mr President, lick my dick hole, bastard bitch!"

That was it. Our legs fell away and we hit the deck laughing. Stomach crunching – jaw aching – pant pissing laughter. Alvan was the best. He had the best insults. He called Mr Reeves 'bitch son of a cum-eater' once and Mr Reeves almost hit him and we all had to stop behind after school because he caused a laughter riot.

"Yo' know what IT is? Do ya?" Nick turned to Alvan.

"I do, yeah. I've done it."

"Well, go on then," I said. "What is it?"

38

"You take your dingy and put it in the woman's thingy."

"What the fuck!"

"That's mental!"

We spent the rest of the summer in our sukkah. We drew treasure maps we never used. Planned war missions we never went on. Built a cart we only rolled out once. The moms let us sleep in it a couple of times. We were old enough to know, too young to think it through.

"'Ad a good sleepover, lad?" Dad asked me.

"Good, ar. Mrs Maleh med us them sticky cakes again."

"'Er's a good sort for a darky, that wench is." He laughed at himself. "So whatcha gerrup to?"

"Well," I said. "We made a few decisions about things."

"Oh ar? Sounds like big plans."

"It is ar. We've decided we ay gerrin married an' 'avin' kids. Weem gonna be a gang in our sukkah when we grown up. Alvan says he knows how to grow veg and milk goats. Nick'll be our cleaner an' arm the guard."

"Is that so?" Dad chuckled. "Yo' ay gerrin married or nothin' an yo'm livin' with the boys, an' yo'm . . . yo'm security?"

"Thass right."

Mom came in the kitchen just as Dad said that. "I'll remind yo' 'a this when yo'm older," she said.

"I wo' need remindin', Mom."

All of this came out about fifteen years later when Alvan was Nick's best man. Some of it's buried though. Deep. Old enough to know. Too young to think it through.

———————

"I'll show you," Alvan said. "Get your dick out."

"Fuck off yo' gaylord," Nick said.

"Scared," Alvan said.

"I ay scared," I said standing up. I pulled my tracksuit trousers down and got it out.

"Bummers!" Nick said.

Then Alvan stepped towards me and he pulled the front of his tracksuit bottoms down and pulled his cock over the waistband. It was different. He had dark skin over his and the end of it had no skin at all – just a weird purplish blob with a red rim and a blowhole. And he stood right up next to me and he pulled his out and he got mine and he made them kiss. He made mine snuggle into his. Nick just sat with his gob open. And I looked at Alvan and he was smiling, his pale blue eyes beaming and wide, and I went a little dizzy, but it was a nice kind of dizzy, like when Dad's car goes too fast over the humps in the road. Alvan made our dicks kiss a couple of times. And our willies sort of cried and it was nice but it was shivery. And then I felt that twinge. I felt the redness. I felt odd. I was clear, raged. I couldn't help myself. Like that night, much later, when I was up on the reservoir. Like the times I went through my Naval stuff or the Dudley News or sharpened my blades. Then

40

I pushed him away and kicked him in his chest and he lost his breath. Nick laughed a bit and I threw my shoe at him.

"Fuckin' gay halal queer," I said. Then we laughed. Nick tried it with him the night after and this time no one got upset. We were old enough to know. We were too young to think it through.

Laurel Road

The wench on Laurel Road was as old as the road. You'd see her walk to and from Bennett's Butchers on a Tuesday morning. I say walk – she was crippled over with C-shaped spine, calves swollen and pink, root paths of blue worm veins. You'd only see her on a Tuesday. She stank of soil and piss and carbolic soap. Folk round here gave her a wide berth.

The rest of her week she tended her garden. She'd planted conifers at the boundary, so no one knew what she was doing but she brought jams and pickles and giant vegetables to the fete and Farooq lived two doors up and he said his mom said she was always dropping off carrots and spinach and stuff. Farooq went missing years later, just after the last night of service at The Caves pub.

You'd only see her on a Tuesday. Hobbling. Staring at the floor. She'd phlegm-cough, hawk and spit. Seemed a bit proud of it too. Noble even.

"Eh up, 'ere comes the Laurel Witch," Mom'd say.

"Er looks good for 'er age," Dad'd joke. "Hope I'm that active when I'm hundred and forty."

Burroughs lived up Laurel Road too. Prick, he was. His home was cut back from the road – a line of five bungalows. Way back in primary school, before he got massive, stubbled and did try outs at the Villa, we still spoke to him a bit then. He told us about her one Monday at wet playtime.

"Listen," he said. "On Sunday I sid the Laurel Witch."

We were stunned. All games stopped. All the drawing and snakes and ladders paused.

"My brother threw my red power ranger gun over 'er garden," he said.

Big Burroughs was a prick too. He was about seven years older than us, so he was already selling weed up on the basketball courts when we were still playing war in the woods. He'd been in and out of the cells and each time he did he looked a little bit angrier, a little bit more afraid. Nick told me he heard Big Burroughs talking about the prison gangs and how the gangs on our estate were the same. He seemed to think that one of the reasons so many of them settled on the Wrenna was because they wanted revenge on him. Pete day think so, but I thought about it when the bill went through the house of Lords and became a Law. This new bloke from the council had come on the Central News and was talking about how these ex-prisoners had served their time with all the broken promises and missed opportunities that society had doled out.

"They hand out these books," Burroughs'd said. "An' they section us all off in different groups an' these gangs get taught, brainwashed, armed. They wo' be in theya forever."

He was right.

"You know my brother," Burroughs started. "'E's bigger than my dad and they'd both lamp me if I started blartin on, and Mom'd be furious so I 'opped over the fence and crawled through the branches. 'Er grows veg an' stuff in every bit of her garden. 'Er ay got lawn or nothing."

We were fixed. Everyone knew the Laurel Witch. Some of us called her a hag. Nan called her Daphne. Everyone knew her one way. We were fixed to her by stories. We were repelled by the stories. They run like vines through every stretch of the estate.

"So I was searching 'er beds," Burroughs said. "An' ferreting through the cabbages an' stuff. On my knees an' fingering at the ground. An' 'round the end 'a the cucumber patch . . . there 'er was."

Burroughs told us how she lifted him up by the ear. Pulled him into the house.

"'Er sat me down an' 'er stood right in front 'a me. 'Er put 'er donnies on me shoulders and 'er spoke."

"When you're caught in that night-time-scape," 'er said, the witch did, day 'er. "In dreams. Where you run but can't run. Where you scream but have no throat. When you're held and your limbs are liquid. When you forgot about the body you'd hidden a few dreams ago. Where you find yourself compromised by a door or a

44

choice. This is where you'll find me – caught in a constant dawn."

She took out this liquid. A small vial with clear, gloopy oil stuff in it. She wiped it on his hair.

"It stuck to me 'air an' me yed," he said. "It sort 'a went sticky an' pale an' a bit lumpy," he said. "Stank 'a soil an' the muck around Green Pool."

Then she let him go and we stopped going up there and Burroughs, prick he was, never lost that habit of checking behind him, never lost the stain of sleeplessness under his eyes. He got bitter and nasty. Never lost those strange eyes. We day speak to him after that.

Wren's Nest Primary School

Mom said when she was pregnant she used to walk through the woods with me in her belly, she used to walk to the local school, and she'd watch the kids in the playground and she used to think about how I might be when I came about.

"I really thought about it, I did," she said. "More than thinkin' really, bab. I saw it in me 'ead. They all thought I was mad, they did. And I think all that thinkin' came through to yo' when yo' was born too, day it? Yo' always 'ad summat. Summat in yower eyes. They all thought I was mad."

"We did, ar," Dad said. "'Er used to gu from our 'ouse through the woods an' up to the school an' 'er'd stand outside an' 'er'd think about yo' an' the school an' 'ow to be a mom."

I used to make Dad read me the Ladybird Book of Custer's Last Stand every night when I was a kid. He'd tuck me in and make a joke about how lanky I was and he'd snuggle up next to me.

"Before they faced the great war he thought of his mother," Dad read. "He thought of all the mothers.

When they had newborns they made up songs and stories and the child was the centre of it. The child was the chorus of our songs. The child was set in the story as the defender of their people."

Me and Nick had been best mates from reception. He was naughty and I loved it. He was the fastest runner and he knew all the swear words and he knew how to get between the school fence and the back of the houses when we played war and his mom used to let us watch Van Damme films. We played war in the woods too. We built dens. It was Nick who taught me how to ride no-hands on my bike. And we helped each other clean our rooms so we could get out quicker and we had more time before it got dark. His dad taught us how to do the Cruyff turn and my dad taught us how to fish and fight.

"The 7th Cavalry worked their way towards them," Dad'd read. "Sitting Bull looked left and right along the line of warriors. The men looked back. At six he was put to work with the men and the men made bonds. Woman and man loved with desire and instinct. Man and man worked at kinship through toil and vow and tests. They would die for their brother through this."

We had Mrs Simpson in year three and she had us do a play for World Book Day. Me and Nick did a fight scene from Custer's Last Stand. Dad used to read it to me – I never let him read anything else, I never let him skip a page, and he tried. I was Sitting Bull – I did a sun dance and talked about soldiers falling like grasshoppers from the sky. It was in assembly, just after hymns and the Lord's Prayer. Mrs Simpson asked us to perform. Nick was Custer and I was Sitting Bull and we'd made our costumes ourselves. We had two lines.

"Your men will fall like grasshoppers from the sky," I said.

"Attack!" Nick said.

We sort of danced it. Slow motion mime. He fired and I rolled. I thrust at him with a plastic spear and he blocked. Slow. Mimed. We kept catching each other's eyes and giggling. The teachers giggled too. Then I tackled him to the floor and I pretended to scalp him. Slow motion mime. Everyone was silent. Wide eyed and mouths open. And it was just a game but I felt that redness and that twinge feeling. Oddness.

"Sitting Bull's Mother and Grandmother taught him to be still and silent. They taught him to speak in low, gentle tones. To speak only what is required. His Father said *nothing has more terror than gentleness*." Dad read. All our dads were the same quiet types and I remembered that when it came time.

We went up to Auntie Carlin's to make our costumes. She had feathers and old leathers. Her house was full of weird stuff.

"'E was called Jumpin' Badger when 'e was a kid," she said. "'E was called Slow too. 'E 'ad to prove 'imself fust. We all 'ave to prove ourselves."

When Alvan moved to the Wrenna we made him jump out of the tallest tree to join in. Me and Nick swam the length of Green Pool without coming up for air. The moms went mad and we had to take our clothes off at the front door and the girls went nuts.

"Go to the Crow, Jumping Badger," Dad did all the different voices, and he'd pull faces for the different Indians. "That's what Chief had said. Leave the women and leave your youth and ride with the warriors. You'll come back a bull. Sitting Bull was only fourteen when he rode out front in the raid and took three heads and two horses. That night his Father gave him the eagle feather and a new name – Thathanjka Iyotake."

Dad had a tattoo across his chest. *Better a warrior in a garden than a gardener in a war.* He knew how to fight but he hardly ever said a word about it. He took me and Nick to Priory Boxing Club. I made him read me Custer's Last Stand every night.

"Put yower skin in the game," 'e told me years later. "When it comes to it, doh 'esitate. Put yower skin in the game."

Willow Road

Dad trained with a Shaolin Monk when he was a young man. He'd gone travelling in the early nineties. Went to China. Met Master Tan.

"You've got to be a reed in the breeze," he said. "A reed in the breeze. I spent six months of a gap year perfecting that."

"Good for you," I told him. He gave me a gentle slap that I never saw coming and a laugh I did.

It was years later. After I'd come back from Portsmouth. I did alright at first in the Navy after the initial shock of training and that first night out on manoeuvres. It was when we got deployed to Helmand that I got ill. I got sent home.

I was walking an old route, as an adult, down Willow Road. A perfect parallel of red-brick terraces tightly set in the narrow street. And the wind was blowing. Blowing like the skimming of a stone, kicking up used cans and chip wrappers.

At the end of the road is a gulley. You've got to go single file, watch for who's coming the other way. The gulley connects Willow Road to Old Park Road, running between the off-licence and the patch of waste ground. That waste ground is covered in weeds and grasses and rodents and bugs. Littered with bricks, tiles and cinder blocks from a few half-attempted builds. The wind in the gulley kicks the dust in your eyes. It'll take your feet from the street.

"You've gotta be a reed in the breeze."

Broom Road

If we were on one end of the woods and we heard Mother Hutton shouting, we used to race each other down to the Post Office where the Wren's Nest Road meets Summer road. I'd go in and ask Mr Patel loads of random questions like *do yo' 'ave Sundee Roasts in Pakistan or is it true yo' all 'ave pet cows* – meanwhile our gang'd rob him blind of sweets and Panda Pop and pornos while he tried to be polite.

So, we'd be up in the woods at the back of Hillside Road and when Mother Hutton's call came we'd race through bramble and birch and jump the fence between the woods and the back gardens. We'd run up the sides of the houses and jump the gates, then race through the gulley to jump the back fences of Broom road then up and over more gates.

"Iss alright fer yo', yo' lanky prick," Nick'd say. "Yo've onny gorra step over the fences."

There was a dog at number four and we used that house because the guy looked like Elvis and he'd go mad and chase us.

"Fuck off, Elvis! Go fuck yower dog."

Elvis kept osses on the brown land by the cut. I never liked the way osses stare at you. They're big and they're pathetic too.

That's where it happened. Broom Road. He was waiting.

Broom Road is the same as the others. Slightly greyed pebbledash houses and surprisingly good gardens. Dog shit, fag butts and special brew cans. They were alright up there. Dad worked with about four of them and they came to Mom's fortieth at the Bramford Arms. But they hated us as kids. *Gu up ya own end!* We trampled the tulips and daffs racing away from Elvis.

Broom Road. I haven't been back. That's where it happened. He was waiting.

"Juno 'utton!" her mom howled, and we legged it down the bank and over the fence into the back gardens of Hillside, then up and over the fronts, then into Elvis' garden and out onto Broom Road. I landed in a puddle as I vaulted the gate – soaked. My trainers sank into the massive puddle, it splashed up to cover back and front. Then it came. Broom Road. He was waiting.

I hadn't landed more than a second. The stagnant water hadn't soaked in yet. He jumped from behind the car and threw a fist at my face. It landed. Not well though. Then another one; better this time. Straight in the jaw. Burroughs.

I saw him and I saw his eyes and he looked pissed and he looked worried too. And he seemed to be studying the dark rims around my eyes. The puddle started to sink through my trousers. Focus. Perfect focus without thought and the blood in the brain and the chill and the shiver and the strange calm. I stood against a decent fist to the jaw – took left foot back, skipped forward, fists raised and struck out. Simple. Focus. Burroughs, prick he was, dropped his guard. Simple – jab, jab, cross. Simple – nose, nose, chin. We drill that every week. He hit the deck. Nose crushed and bleeding. I gave him a kick in the gut. His mates just stood there. Burroughs couldn't breathe. Our lot circled around us. There was that redness again.

"Yo' fuckin' ponned 'im out," Nick said. He jumped up and down in victory.

"Who's not singin', Burroughs?" I said. "Down like a straw man. Pussy!"

Heart race and slight shake, I couldn't stop my head nodding. That twinge. That oddness. Shoulders back and glaring. I looked down on Burroughs. Prick, he was. Slayed. Tamed. That redness and shiver. Looking back I can connect this with fucking and fighting and the Navy and that night up on the reservoir. I nodded to myself. Bit my lip. He was done, beat back, snapped – I'd tamed him. The corners of my mouth curled. He was collared.

Burroughs' breath gargled in gasps – snorting on blood. I went for one more but got pulled back. One heavy hand on my shoulder.

"Lerrit gu, youngun. Iss done," Elvis said. Pulled me back and stood between us. "Gerrim outta 'ere," he said to Burroughs' crew.

"We ay 'is mate," one said.

"Doh show yower face," I said as he got to his knees. "We've all 'ad enough. Iss yower fault. Yo'm a prick, ay ya? An you've bin a prick to us all. Alright? Petal 'ead."

Elvis pulled me back again and the rest of the guys skulked off. Burroughs got himself up. Wiped his nose and looked up at me. I'd never seen his eyes like this before. I'd never seen-seen them. Great big eyes. Eyes like osses. Big watery brown eyes. Begging eyes. He turned and walked off. His shoulders sunk and mine mirrored them.

"Fuck off then," Elvis said to me. He sort of looked like he was going to spit.

Celandine Road

When I came home from the Navy, Dad'd already died and I hadn't seen Mom for about year. I wasn't myself at first – something about moving back and something about those nights out in Helmand Province. I stayed away at first. I had a strange twitch in my arm. I was always thirsty and I could never sleep.

Mom hugged me and made tea. She really did hug me. She did a twirl in her Help the Heroes hoodie. She raised and dropped her eyebrows a few times as she held my arms and tapped her palm against my torso.

"Day yo' get fed in the Navy?" She asked. She hugged me. Then she said:

"Nicky Culpepper says, 'er says, 'er ay sat down for wik. I says why, I says an' I thought 'er'd bin busy with 'er grandkids an' doin' shifts up Cedar Road again. No, 'er says, 'er says 'er ay sat down 'cause of 'er piles. I'm covered, 'er says, them all over me bum 'ole, 'er says. An' yo' know wharr'er's like, doh ya, 'er ay never shy is 'er? an' like our Nan used to say, er'd say 'er never less the truth gerr'in the way of a good yarn, does 'er, 'er'd say, 'er did."

"So, I was theya, we were in the kitchen, we was, yo' know 'ow me an' some 'a the wenches meetup on a Wednesdee, yo' do, yo' know, we 'ave coffee an' our Jean'll mek a cake or Nicky Culpepper'll get 'er best biscuits out. Yo' know. Anyroad, I was theya an' there was just me an' 'er this wik. Jean was at the clinic, did I tell yo' 'er's 'ad a date for 'er last session 'a chemo? I did, ar. God 'elp 'er. Thass why we started doin' the coffee mornins, we did, for Jean, we did. Yo' used to fancy 'er Laura, day yo', day yo' gu out with 'er a couple 'a times? Yo' did ar. 'Er's got twins with that lad from down the Fox an' Grapes now. Yo' know 'im, yo' do, yo' do, yo' went to cubs with 'im. Yo' do. That coulda bin yo' that could. God bless 'em. Them a lovely family."

"Anyway, I thought Nicky Culpepper, yo' know 'er doh yo, yo' do ar, yo' do, I thought 'er'd 'ave me listen to all that tripe about 'er grandkids an' 'er shifts an' all that. An' yo' know 'ow 'er gus on and on an' 'er doh leave a breath to breathe or ask yo' ow yo'm doin, er doh. If 'er knew better 'er'd probably do better but 'er doh. I thought it'd be another big speech, like. But no, 'er says iss piles, 'er says, 'er's covered in em. An' the next thing yo' know 'er's gorr'er knickers round 'er ankles an' 'er yed between 'er legs, an' er's talkin' to me, 'er is, talkin' upside down, 'er is. Er's 'oldin' the back of 'er legs an' 'er's talkin to me, 'er is. An' 'er bum's in the air – facin' straight at me, it is, an' 'er's talkin' upside down, 'er is. 'Er says, 'ave yo' ever sid anythin' like that, 'er says. I've sid some stuff in my life, as yo' know, yo' doh do twenty years as a community nurse

57

on the Wrenna without learnin' a few things about folk. But this. Blood 'ell, bab. Yo' couldn't see 'er bum 'ole for the red raw warts, yo' couldn't. Looked like a donut, it did. I tell a lie, it looked like a donut med 'a that funny red sausage yower red Russian mate ates."

"Polish Pete?" I asked.

"Thass 'im. 'Ere, day 'e 'ave some gypsy cure for yo' that once? Yo' know. Down theya. 'E did, ar."

I sneezed tea out of my nostrils. Mom was pointing at my crotch and doing her eyebrow bounce. There's nothing people don't find out about.

"So I says, I does, I says Nicky Culpepper yo' get yower knickers up an' yo' talk to me like yow'd talk to any other mon or wench, I ay yower nurse no more, I says. An' 'er just stood theya. Froze, er was. Yed upside down an' gooin' red. Bum in the air. Just stood theya. So I left, I did."

We ate cod roe an' shared a bag of chips that night. We had a can of bitter shandy and watched Strictly. Mom'd say, "mek em wait an' they wo' do nothin', mek 'em wait an' remember what yower old mon tode yo'."

Not long after this me and our Caz 'ad to feed her with a syringe.

Summer Road

I walked past decayed buildings, desolate public houses and ruined walls. Cranes pierced the skyline. Yawning upwards, towards grey clouds. Then plunged deep into the earth, screwing into the soils. Cogs turned cogs, grating chains that spiralled coils and spasmed the ground. Metal beasts pulling down the mills, building temples for shiny shoed suits to live. Garden City they call it. Our dads used to work there. In the short years between my Navy service and returning home, so much had been demolished and renovated.

I pass rustling waste and rotting sanitary towels. Fences guard the sites with wrought iron vigilance. Axles and beer cans rust in the ruin. The gangs have bought up patches of this land and they are sitting on it.

Wrenna windows witness screams of smog and sunlight. Towering red brick chimneys and dark church spires catch dust. In almost-identical streets, children drink cans of full proof liquor, families rage war and slate grey tiles cuddle together. Things have changed. Only the bookies does any business on the Wrenna these days.

Between fried food bonanzas, clock in clock out and sleep, people shout, starve, stone the family pet. They laugh a little, eyes rolling backwards. Shrug. Cries are heard among the cogs and chains, the flames and shouts, the revs, the screeches.

Dog shit and chewing gum scar the streets. Window boxes wilt where paint cracks, revealing bones, old tissues and soggy cardboard.

I thought about all of this from the reservoir all those years later. The blood. The sack. Struck in a stare.

A dog lies panting on the pavement. I slowly lower myself. Grit and broken glass dig into my knees and arms. I feel the wet tarmac slowly soak through my t-shirt and spread across my chest. Summer Road's litter glitters in the sun. My cheek, chest, arms and legs are grounded in this beautiful filth. I turn my face to meet the dog's weeping eye and it rests its paw on my shoulder, its breath ragged. I stroke its balding mane. We stare at each other. The church bell tolls out. All goes silent. The dog dies with a slow exhale.

Linden Road

I reckon all of us are built with a ton of different stuff. We're part fact and part fiction. All of it's real.

Dr Kaur lived on Linden Road and she was our doctor from birth. She had a house out in Edgbaston too, a big, detached place with a drive and privet bushes and a garage and she had one of them stone pizza ovens in her garden, but she kept this house for weekends. Every weekend she'd look after Mr Patel, who refused to move from the Wrenna, even though every generation of child in every house on the estate had screwed him one way or another.

"This is my home," Mr Patel said. "I've got through the antics of enough nutjobs and this lot are no different." This lot *were* different though. These gangs. They roamed, they lurked. They were organised.

They took their front gardens really seriously on Linden Road. They still cleaned their doorsteps. Every year, Mom made us go up and give Dr Kaur a thank you card on my birthday. Proper bed-wetter, Mom was. Dr Kaur'd make us tea and we'd have them funny paki sweets.

"They 'ad no bed for us," Mom'd say. "We 'ad to sleep in the 'ospital 'all."

"Like Jesus," I said, and they all rolled their eyes again.

"When I first saw yo'," Nan'd say – she said it all the time – "I came up Russell's Hall with yower Granddad. Look arrim, Stan, I said, look arrim. Boster, ay 'e, yower Grandad said, 'e did. An' yo' were, yo' were. Yo' 'ad muscles an' dimples, yo' did."

"Like Hercules," I said and they all rolled their eyes again.

"Like Siegfried," Dad'd say, and he'd wink.

"An' yo' looked up at me," Nan'd say. "Yo' did, yo' looked up with them big funny eyes." And Nan'd stretch her eyelids out as she spoke. "Day 'e, cock? 'E 'ad massive sunken eyes, day 'e? An' yo looked up at me an' I swear on Granddad's grave yo' looked an' looked again. Like yo' knew me."

"Like Sam Beckett," Dad'd say, and only he laughed.

"An' I said, I said, 'e's bin 'ere afore 'e 'as, ay 'e?"

"Like Sam Beckett," Dad'd say.

Dr Kaur was young looking, even though she'd been around us all our lives. She was little and she wore smart clothes and you'd hear her listening to Ed Sheeran on her car radio. She'd roll her eyes at me and smile, and she'd giggle at Dad's one liners, and she'd hang on Mom and Nan's every word. Everyone in the Spills Meadow'd raise a glass to her on New Years, Christmas, and we'd take those smelly candles round to her and Mr Patel. We never figured out if he was her proper uncle, but she called him Chacha, and it was only ever the two of them.

"Dr Kaur," Mom'd start. "D'yo remember the fust time we tried to wash 'im?"

Dr Kaur smiled and nodded, and she gave me a look and she gave Dad one too.

"I still day know 'ow to 'old 'im proper. Show me, I said, day I, I said. An' yo' day either, did yo, Dr Kaur, did yo'?" Dr Kaur smiled and nodded.

"Not that yo' day know," Mom'd say. "Yo' know, yo just day see this un comin' did yo'? Bloody wriggle this way an' wriggle that way, day 'e? Wi' 'is lanky limbs. 'E did, ar. Like a bloody carp or summat, I said, day I, I did. 'E's like a bloody carp, I said, I did."

Everyone laughed. Every year. And Dad'd pull me out of my seat and dangle my arms around like I was his puppet.

"'E's still the sem," Dad said. "Still a stick insect. Still cor gerrim in the bath."

Everyone laughed. Every time.

"All we could do," Dr Kaur said. "Was grab you by the arms and dip you in the sink, and you'd wriggle. And we'd have to turn you around and dip another bit in. And you'd wriggle. And we'd never be able to get your left foot in. There was always one little bit on your ankle."

"Thass what that smell is?" Dad'd say.

Everyone laughed. Every year. Every time.

And I remember this. I think. I mean, I kind of half remember and some of it's changed and some of the

63

gaps are filled in by what Nan says or what Mom says or the little looks Dr Kaur gives me. But I do remember.

One year, around the time I'd pushed Burroughs over at the fete, Olwen was at Dr Kaur's too. Nan'd bought her along.

"He's always tried to wriggle out of stuff," Olwen said.

And we all kind of looked at each other in silence for a few seconds and then we pretended she'd said nothing. Except Nan. Nan smiled, stroked Olwen's hair and tapped her on the knee. Nan looked at me too, then back at Olwen and pulled that odd face she did when she thought a girl was pretty.

Olwen called me *Culhwch* sometimes and I thought it was a welsh swear word.

Lavender Road

"Am yo' guin up the laundrette?" the lads'd say. "Off te see the washerwomen, am ya?"

That's what we'd say. That's what we'd call them. Washerwomen. The whores at number twenty-eight. It was like a code, but one everyone knew. More manners than code, I suppose. Like saying *I'm guin to the toilet* even though everyone knows you're saying, *I'm avin a shit.*

Rati was my favorite. Sometimes we'd just talk. She'd come over from Australia and she used to call us POMs and she went a bit nuts once when I told her –

"POM means Prisoner of Motherland, so . . . erm . . . yo'm the fucking POM, bitch."

I found out over the years that her parents grew up in Bilston, moved out to Adelaide in the nineties and then came back with her about ten years later, so she wasn't even a real Aussie, and I was never convinced her real name was Rati.

None of us really believed. You never admitted to believing. We all watched Candyman too early when we were kids and we knew it was saft but we never did the chant in the mirror. The older kids'd make up stories about Lavender Road and doing weird stuff.

"'Er let me landshark 'er."

"The old wench'll give yo' a ballcuzzi."

We never believed it. We never admitted to believing it. It was like the dads telling us about the grey woman down the Coseley Tunnel. Or Nan and her tales about Bella and the Wych-Elm. Stories get under your skin though. They fester.

The first time I went up Lavender Road I was seventeen. I picked Rati out of the line-up. I had to walk up the end of my road and walk around the estate the wrong way, like I was heading to college or to town and I had to keep checking behind me and my head was cold and my neck was tight and I kept checking my nostrils with my sleeve. I had three cigarettes and a packet of herbals. I went down past Priory Boxing and cut back towards Lavender Road that way. Turned my jacket inside-out. I yawned and shivered and there was a tight pulse in my throat. I walked past number twenty-eight three times. The fourth time there was a wench at the door.

"Business?"

Fuck me, them real!

"Sorry, what?"

"Any business?"

"Oh . . . erm, no thank you."

"'Ave a good day then, bab."

"Sorry, what?"

"'Ave a good day."

"Oh . . . erm, yeah. Thank you. You too."

The first time I really went I was eighteen. I still had that throat pulse. Shivers. Yawns. I picked Rati out of the line-up. They had slightly larger semi-detached homes up there, with the same off-cream, slightly riffy facades. The front room was made out like any other lounge – a three-piece suite and a television, pictures of family members and knick-knacks on the faux fireplace. Four wenches stood in front of me and the older one asked me who I wanted. Rati was pale and tall with bright blue eyes and short cropped blonde hair. Beautiful. I picked Rati. I'd done *it* before, but I wanted to do it this way too. I wanted to pay. I wanted to feel a bit dirty. I wanted a washerwoman. She led me up the stairs. Wooden ornaments and stone figures ran along the windowsill and flatpack shelves. Weird figures. You'd see them in the hippy shops in Stourbridge or Worcester. The house smelled of incense and harvests at Uncle Bill's farm. She led me into the first room at the top. It was cold. Clinical. Just a bed, drawn curtains, plastic sheet covers. I sat on the bed – plastic crackle.

"You're really slim," she said. "Athletic."

My cock got hard when she slotted the latch across the lock – clicked into place with a swift wrist flex. It cost thirty quid and she fucked my brains out for forty seconds.

Sometimes she gave me a discount and sometimes we'd just talk. We'd sit on her bed and she'd make tea. She taught me things.

When I was twenty-something I'd come back from Pompey on shore leave and I paid just to go down on her. I pushed her to the bed and pulled her dressing gown apart, gently bent one leg up and drew it out at the knee, then slowly did the same to the other, got to my knees and began. She held the back of my neck with pincer grip, subtly tilting my head this way and that, arching pelvis and rubbing clit over roaming tongue. I pushed my face into the warm flesh. Felt her legs that viced my face quiver slightly, tense, then relax. I sucked. Ran the edge of my tongue over that glistening kitzler.

"You know," I said. "The Greeks called it a key. The key."

"Fuck off," she said and gave my cock a little shake.

And sometimes I'd get her to hit me and sometimes I tied her up. Sometimes we'd get Christine involved, and sometimes I just watched. Sometimes it was animal, and fucking was the same as sparring at the gym, and sometimes it flowed softly, and sometimes she made tea and we'd just talk. And the talking helped as much as the fucking.

"There's been three, maybe four over all these years that got a bit rough," she told me. "Most punters are really nice. Gentlemen, I suppose. They see it for what it is. I see it for what it is. I think the wenches on the streets get it harder than us – pardon the pun."

She offered me a garibaldi from a plate. I always thought that was odd – a polite perversity.

"People get hung up on it," Rati said. "Men come and

see me because I'm fucking hot. That's nice. It's nice to be hot. Nice that people think so. People think men only see hotness. Like they walk around all day with hard-ons and no other thought."

I took a garibaldi. Left it on my tongue to melt.

"See, this is a place for sex, right?" she asked.

"Thass right, ar," I said.

"People, men, come here to get laid, or to do something along the lines of getting laid, right?"

"Thass right, ar."

"And even in this place we get people like you."

"Wass that meant to mean?" I asked, looking up from the plate, eyebrows low.

"It means, my little panda-eyed boy, that even in a place like this, they still come here with other things to do and say and other things on their minds. It's not just fucking."

"No, thass true."

"So, how does that play out in the rest of the world? In the real world? Some people think they're all just lying around their filthy bedsits wanking themselves raw, breaking their backs trying to get the end of their cocks in their mouths." I laughed. Spat some part-liquified garibaldi on her knee. She scraped it off with a smirk.

"I've had worse things land on me, babe."

She plucked another biscuit and posted it between my lips. Gave me a kiss. Then started folding up the bedsheets.

"Same with yo'," I said. "What people think, I mean. I think you could give great head AND you could read a book too."

She stared at me for a few seconds. I got that shiver, and that cold to hot, and that throat-pulse. Then she smirked. She punched me on the arm and giggled. Then I laughed. I helped her into her dressing-gown before I left.

———————

There was a welsh chap – or was he scouser – called Niall, and he said, *I went in a kid wanting to feel filthy. I came out surprisingly clean.* I thought about that years later up at the reservoir. Thought about the cold water and the filthy blood and being cleansed.

———————

After Dad died I moved back on the Wrenna to help our Caz look after Mom. I went to see Rati every month or so. She got older but those blue eyes didn't. Her skin creased slightly but her limbs were still supple. Eventually, once the gangs found a footing, the washerwomen were got rid of.

"I'm moving back to Adelaide," she told me the last time. "My brother's killed himself."

We knew five men between us who'd done the same.

Hillside Road

In the dream you saw the trim, slender, stockinged legs of tall schoolgirls. Dark opaque pillars tightly holding in their virtue. These pillars beg – to be looked at, to be touched. You look up to see a smile and mocking eyes. These girls line up – strutting past you. They line up – sitting on the high brick walls where legs dangle. You look – following the regiment of those faces with fingers waving left, then right, heads slightly tilted. They know it all and they won't move. And that is what gives them such a pull.

You continue. Rushing. The saliva will not rest and you can smell it. You continue. Pacing quickly past derelict buildings, all boarded up, windows empty, only darkness and dust, the occasional piece of unused furniture.

Dudley Chronicle

Missing person investigation launched in search of Dudley Teen.

DETECTIVES have launched a missing person's investigation after a 14 year old girl was reported missing in Dudley yesterday. The girl from Wren's Nest was last seen leaving Russell's Hall hospital with serious injuries following a previous report of domestic abuse. Police have been examining CCTV and carrying out enquiries to try to establish who may have seen her or been involved in her disappearance. Patrols have also been stepped up and officers say they are supporting the family during this difficult time. Detective Inspector Laura Cooper, who is leading the investigation, said: "A young woman is lost and this is a deeply distressing time for her family and friends. We will be working round the clock to establish who was responsible for this and try to understand why it happened. I would urge anyone with information to get in touch as soon as possible."

Anyone with information which can help the police investigation is urged to contact officers via Live Chat, or by calling 101. Quote 30DY/29354Q/21.

Alternatively ring Crimestoppers anonymously.

Spinney

On the cow paths or main routes, your eye might get caught by the chalky yellow of limestone, collected into small piles. I'm not sure how well we remember these things. We'd take the steps down into the umber and tan - the stench of wood rot and new stems. We'd cut through the slade – the coop-caw of pigeon and crow, the scuttle-snaps of rodent. And around a corner – sometimes – the limestone burial mound that wasn't there a week ago and will soon be gone.

Bluebell Road

Every now and then Little Phil turned up. It'd be months between, but you bet if it was our Christie's fiftieth or Nick's stag do, Little Phil'd pop up. No one knew about the pictures except us, but we all knew there was something about him that day sit well.

"'E needs a fuckin' bell 'round 'is neck, doh 'e?"

"'E needs summat 'round 'is neck, thass for sure, bab."

But it was when Mark won the nationals for his marrowfats that it really kicked off. Mark was hard but he was normally newted too. Jackie was his wench. They ran the allotment committee down Bluebell Road. It wasn't a real allotment. They'd taken over a bit of the land the council never got around to building on and no one dared to move them. Jackie had a bit of gypo in her. She had the scars from a childhood rash on her neck. She brewed potato vodka and sloe gin and she handed it out to people she'd only met twice. She'd meet the moms at the Priory Ruins with the kids and take them to see Santa at Dudley Castle and she'd never take a penny off them.

"Iss a treat for me too, bab. Them my babbies too, ay they?"

Dad said, "If yo' ever get to buy Jackie a pint before 'er gess yo' one I'll give yo' me Triumph."

Mark and Jackie came into The Britannia and she gripped his wrist and flung it into the air.

"Best fuckin' pays in show ... gu to ... the Wrenna Boy!"

Mark hung his head and shook it but you could see he was relishing it too. He'd look up from time to time, do a sort of half-shrug-eye-roll, then scan the room to make sure we were all looking.

"Two bitters please, Si," she said.

"On me, these," Si said. "Well done, Mark."

Jackie still paid but Si said he gave her it all back in change and she didn't notice. And I got him one in and so did Alvan and Nick and even Flo did, and he was tight as badger's arse.

"Fuckin' 'ell Flo, is it a Leap Year?"

"Gu fuck yourself. 'Ere's to ya, Mark."

The thing with Little Phil was this, everyone knew him but no-one knew-knew him. He'd sort of scrummage his way into groups and conversations. He always found a way in. He always seemed to know something was happening and he'd make his way there. He spoke to everyone and no-one really knew him and he spoke like he really did know them. He never shut up – never knew how to shut up. And we knew more about him than the others. I'd studied those pictures and I'd studied his stare. Years later he stopped shaving and joined the gangs. The thing with Little Phil was he was short. Not just short, really tiny, and his limbs were boyish too. He wasn't a dwarf or nothing. He was a little man. The thing with little Phil was he was riffy – not filthy, just a little dusty. The thing with him was he always looked odd. He always had a strange look about him. A strange look in his eye. A bit like Burroughs, I suppose. He sized you up. Peculiar eyes. He looked right through you.

"Yo' cor tell," Alvan said. "If 'e wants to fight yo' or to fuck yo'."

"'Ow's 'e avoided a lampin'?" I asked.

The thing with Little Phil was he had a jitter about him. A nervous pent-up tick of the lip, tick of the shoulder, tick of the eye. He was always checking over his shoulder. He never knew how to shut up. Never knew when he wasn't welcome. He looked saft when he joined the gangs those few years on, weedy with his wispy beard, but he'd got numbers behind him then.

The Britannia had history. It was warm. Snug. Old farming tools, pottery tankards, black and white pictures of Gornal, brass and leather and old wood. We sat in the corner, Mark and Jackie by the fire. We were raising glasses and taking the piss and laughing. Mom and Dad played crib with Uncle Bill. Si walked around shaking hands, running his mouth about the Wolves between collecting glasses.

"Yo' shoulda sid that brumajum bastard, Handcock," Mark said. "'Is face when 'e sid my marrowfats."

"Like a two-penny hock!" Jackie said.

"Gerrit it up ya, I said to him. Gerrit right up ya," Mark said, uppercutting the air and meeting elbow joint with his other forearm.

"Good on ya, Mark."

"Well," Mark said. "After last year."

"Yeah!" came a noise. And we all turned around. And there he was. Dusty, ticking Little Phil.

"And whaddayo' know?" Jackie said.

"I know," he said, laughing.

"What? Whatcha know?"

"'Is pays," he said, pointing at Mark.

"And?" Jackie was staring right at him – elbows on the table, finger tapping against her pint.

Little Phil looked back at her. Looked like he wanted to fight and looked like he wanted to fuck. Then he twitched – a full eye-mouth-shoulder twitch. Then he looked around. Looked at all of us.

"And?"

"And," he said, turning to Mark. "And yo' need to keep yower wench on a leash."

In half a heartbeat Jackie turned the table on end and flew across at him, tackling him from his stool to the ground. Our drinks scattered and spilled. They were about the same height seeing them like this. She backhanded him, her rings cut into his face. Then she had him in a headlock, pulled him to his feet and dragged him outside.

"Sorry, Si," she said, passing the bar. Si just waved.

We clung to the windows as she threw him to the floor, put one foot on his head and one finger in his mouth and began to pull at the cheeks. And I gawped with wide gob and I got that odd feeling – the redness and shiver, the thirst and twinge. And thought about that years later, on the reservoir with the hessian sack and blood stains. We couldn't hear her but we saw her lips moving and her face wild. She let him go. Gave him a kick goodbye.

"Watcha say to him, Jackie?" I asked.

"I told him he owes us all a round 'a drinks," she laughed. She took her seat again. "And he agreed."

Not long after Little Phil joined the gangs, he got his revenge and he fought and fucked a few of our Wrenna crew.

Wren's Nest Community Centre

Polish Pete ran the Karate club on Thursday nights. He'd done service before he moved to the Wrenna. I went down to watch one night. Thought I could help him. Some of the girls had already started to go missing and the kids had stopped playing in the woods. These gangs had begun cropping up all over the estate. A few at a time as their different sentences got reduced, and cellmate after cellmate followed each other down to the Wrenna. I thought about Dad and Custer's Last Stand. I'd seen things in the Navy. These gangs were small, but they had weight. Polish Pete knew, he told us when we were kids.

"Cześć, Brother," he said. "I'll teach the kids the things I got taught in the Grom back in Poland, yes, and you can teach them some of your Navy stuff, yes?"

"Sounds good, Pete, ar."

He pulled his bottom lip up over his top, frowned and nodded.

"You hear about Juno?" he asked.

"No, wass up?"

"Nie jest zły! She celebrates."

"Oh ar?"

Pete held out his arms and grinned. Motioned me to stay still.

"She celebrates," he said. "She has now an MPQ."

"An NVQ?" I laughed.

"In pet caring."

I laughed again.

"Good yes," he agreed. "We will be opening a centre for dog cares."

I smiled. Thought about Juno and the flowers and those tits and the way she gripped my hips as we fucked and how she dug fingers into my collarbone, and she could get her grip around my wrist as she pinned me down and how she shivered when she came and how she bit me. Everyone thought she was just a slut. She was more than a slut. "Good for her," I said. "So she's out celebrating?"

"She went to Sedgley Beacon with her sister and they crawling home with the pints."

"I'll get her one in at the Spills," I said.

Then he took his giant step forward and his giant arms wrapped around me and he pulled me in, and he whispered something to me but the hot breath and the accent made me miss it. He grabbed me by the shoulders and stared at me. Eyebrows raised and smiling. I smiled and nodded back. He nodded too. I never found out what I'd agreed to. And I thought about all of this, struck in the stare of that redness, that twinge. I was clear, raged, I couldn't help myself that night up on the reservoir.

Laburnum Road

I went up to see him at the half-way house in Langley. He'd lost the wildness in his eyes. They were glazed, sedated. He was always odd but there was always life there too. He told me about his dreams. A few nights before, he'd startled from a dream with a pain in his eye. In the dream there was nothing. Just himself, somewhere unknowable. At no space or time – just a dark cranny. There was nothing but him and a fork. Not a figurative fork – a literal, eat with a fork-fork. And for a moment or millennia that was all. All was motionless, timeless – a void.

This was a one off, but I remember it really well. We had just passed Top Church on the way home. It was midmorning, a Monday. There were no lectures until late afternoon. Me and Lee left college early. Lee was odd but it was me who followed him into the church. Me who walked down the aisle to the middle. It was me who shimmied with him across the row to the centre of the pew. It was me who pretended to pray.

"What are we doing?" I whispered.

He looked across at me, his hair slightly covering his face. Wild, wide brown eyes and a smirking mouth. I watched him unzip his fly and pull out his cock. And I watched him start to piss on the floor.

The church was silent and empty. The vicar shuffled in his black cassock by the font at the back. The drip and hiss and spray echoed as it tumbled to the sacred boards. I couldn't move, I just watched him. I held my breath and clenched my fingers together. Eyes scrunched tightly closed. Shiver. Twinge. When he stopped we stood and casually walked out of the church.

"Go in the peace of the Lord," the vicar said.

"Thank you," Lee said. We skipped out.

I let out a short sharp breath and Lee fell about laughing. That was the break in the dam. He'd use piss as a weapon for a long time to come.

———

I went up to see him at the half-way house in Langley. There was a milky look to him now. He told me about his dreams. And in the dream he was suddenly surrounded by shit. Soaked, he sat in a brown puddle of it, wet and stinking. He pulled out the fork, held it in front of him and stuck it straight into his eye. That's when he woke up.

Lee had once taken Juno out to a restaurant in Birmingham when she'd split with Polish Pete again. The waitress had questioned his choice of sorbet.

"It'd been a good meal," he said. "A great meal. They served us well and the food was great. There was one thing – an old man having some trouble with his heart and being carted off in an ambulance. But other than that. We had a top meal out."

When it came to ordering pudding, the waitress offered them Lemon, Passion fruit and Apple Sorbets.

"I'll 'ave opple please," Juno said.

The waitress screwed up her face and let out a tut with the suck of her lips. "Erm . . . I said Apple."

"Opple," Lee said in a low whisper and he looked at her, hair partially covering his face. His wild, wide brown eyes. "We'll both 'ave opple."

She smiled and shrugged and left the table.

Then, so he tells me, it occurred to him. He left enough money for the bill on the table. Then stood and went over to the corner of the restaurant, unzipped his fly and began to piss over the floor.

"I was quite casual about it," he said. "Let it out all over the marble tiles."

He then readjusted and walked out of the place with a smile and a nod to the waitress.

Lee told me this one night up his, on Laburnum Road.

"Thing is," I said. "The older we get the more impact these things 'ave. As a teenager yo' might pass it off as 'igh-jinks, but whoever sid yo' this time would've thought – either 'e's mentally ill or incredibly angry."

It was years later at a party Lee's sister was having. I was back home on shore leave. Not a party, a gathering. Almost a wake. She'd had trouble with him over the years. Real fucked up trouble. I vaguely remember swaying in the middle of the street, up on Laburnum Road, holding out my fist, gripping a bottle of vodka. I remember raising it just after the news came in about that old fool being sent down.

"Here's to you, Lee Benton!"

'Local music teacher jailed for hidden camera scandal.'

Lee had been filming kids at school when they went to the toilet. He'd had a series of pupils during band practice and filmed them when they left for a break. He'd taken the music department on trips to York and Swanick. He'd been in charge of the children and then filmed them. Filmed them pissing and shitting and everything. He had a whole catalogue.

I went up to see him at the half-way house in Langley. He told me about his dreams. In his dream he was ashamed. He was disgusted. Covered in filth and the filthy thoughts. Stinking in the shit and the guilt and the shame. He was saturated. And in this stench was an emptiness. His guts gargled and groaned. As if his inside was sucking in at itself – and he enjoyed this. A hungry sensuality.

Old Park Road

I felt fine at the beginning, when we were in training (other than my hatred of that officer with the stick up his backside)! The navy looked after me. We did Cyprus and the Falklands, and it was great. We kept watch. We built schools. We spent a few years taking down Argentinian drug pushers.

I never played AWOL. I had a proper sickness. Even when I went to the fair that night on leave in Pompey. I went alone and came back to the barracks alone. The other guys went to town to fight and fall in love and fuck and vomit on the streets. I was alone at the fair and I wanted to go home. I wanted to go home-home. Back to the Wrenna. I could see something bad was coming.

The next day I was shipped out.

Explosions in the daylight and explosions at night. No sleep. Hiding and waiting and looking down the barrel. That redness. Sweating and cold – we all continued into the desert. The cries of the maimed. The tears. That oddness. I still dream about bits of limb and gut strewn on streets. And I thought about it again that night up at the reservoir. That twinge. I thought about it all as I opened the hessian sack. Surrounded by the chatter of guns and the dust and the smoke, I looked across to the lad I'd gone through basics with. His eyes looked too pale for life and he'd stopped blinking. He stared at me and in his eyes I could see that my eyes were too pale and still as well. He pointed down at the blooded bits of boys that had burst across the ground. "Is he one of ours or one of theirs?" he said.

I was clear, raged. I couldn't help myself. Like that night when I was up on the reservoir. Like the times I went through my Naval stuff or the Dudley News or sharpened my blades.

All this gave my face a new stare. I didn't believe in what I was doing and I wanted to go home. We came out of the desert and found buildings; factories. At midnight we made our break. Within seconds of being in there I knew it was a mistake. We hadn't been given the right equipment, and the comms between the teams was useless, and the enemy gave no fucks, and they didn't have pale still eyes like us. They had dark focussed stares.

I checked through the binoculars just after the airstrike. Looked down from the desert hills and into the village. Out of the grainy cloud that swept between the buildings a young teenage boy came. Scrawny and covered in debris and marked with cuts and blisters. He stepped out into the middle of the street with a machete in his hand and started collecting the heads of the half-dead with swift strikes of his blade. And I packed his machete away in my gear after we'd removed him. And I thought about that as I reached under my bed years later. I was clear, raged. I couldn't help myself. Sharpened my blades.

I came back to Old Park Road just after Dad died. I thought about Custer and Sitting Bull and I thought about the Shaolin Monks. I stayed indoors for a few months. Caz had Mom to look after and told me to suck it up and crack on with it. There was a twitch in my arm I couldn't shake, and I had half-way dreams. I didn't play AWOL but ... There are still lads out there now.

Mon's Hill / Wren's Hill Road

The road sign is different to the name we call it. We call it Mon's 'ill. There's space up here where the trees didn't grow and where they've just started building. It's where the Caves Pub used to be. It's where the gangs moved in. I sat by the window on a Saturday, supping a pint, watching the races, reading the Dudley News. We were close to the end of the local papers then. We weren't to know. I'd read the news and think about what would go through these people's heads, these people that did these things, and I really could see it and read it and hear their thoughts like I did when we were kids on Harebell Crescent. When we broke into number thirteen and I found the photos.

She swung, wearing a red and white dress, and it swung as she did. A makeshift swing made of old rope and a scrapped truck's tyre. Crouching and peering, I sucked my teeth and stared. She had ashen skin and pale green eyes. She smiled as she swung, I imagined she did, tossing her legs back and forth. In her hand were daffodils, necks hung over and strangled in a clenched fist, stems crushed against the tatty rope.

The ground was covered with the cobbles and bricks of the ruined factory. There was nothing else. And no one else. Her friends had been called in for tea already, but her parents were always late. Their dads had had to find work in the city since the gates were shut here and hers had gone further out to find his work. You could still make out the lines where the foundations had been and where the chimney used to plague the sky. The children used the ruins as the grounds of a castle; boys with sticks for guns and girls casting fairy spells out across the estate.

Crouching and peering, I covered my head with a duffle coat hood. The red and white dress wisped and blew, revealing pale limbs with yellow bruises. I imagined her smiling.

I scrambled over the crooked cobbles, sucking my teeth. I looked around – nothing but a concrete no man's land.

She sings a song and swings. And I come from behind.

———

I finished my pint. I shook the thoughts from my mind. She was the first of the girls to go missing. The first to be reported in the newspaper. I thought about Custer and Sitting Bull and I thought about the Shaolin Monks. *Better a warrior in a garden than a gardener in a war.* That's what Dad had tattooed across his chest.

Mom'd say, *mek em wait an' they wo' do nothin', mek 'em wait an' remember what yower old mon tode yo'.* I was clear, raged. I couldn't help myself. Like that night when I was up on the reservoir. Like the times I went through my Naval stuff or sharpened my blades. I think the Dudley News had about three more weeks then until it croaked.

Maple Road

There was this bloke the kids used to laugh at. Dave. You'd see him stumbling along the streets. See him muttering to himself.

Dad said, "stay away from that bloke, I doh like the way he looks at our kids."

Mom said, "'e's alright, 'e's just on 'is own, ay 'e?"

Nan said, "Dave's never done no one any 'arm, no one really knows 'im, mind."

You'd see him stumbling around the estate. Always half drunk, muttering. The type of bloke who couldn't grow a beard but never shaved, wore shoes that were once smart, with a tracksuit. Alvan's Mom used to make pin money clearing people's houses out. She told us about some of the stories she'd found doing Dave's house out.

————

Dave looked up at the clock. It was morning – his birthday. *I'm sixty-eight.* And he picked up the bottle with the three-day old dregs of cider and drained it in two gulps. *I'm gonna to go to the sea. I really need to go to the sea. Which sea is it yo' see in Burnham?*

He arched his back and dug his heels into the mattress – stretched – rocked – jumped out of bed. He stumbled the stairs the way a toddler does. Heavy heeled, heading down. Gripping to the walls, pulling himself into a fall.

Thud! Down the stairs, neck and back arched over. Thud-thud-thud – legs straining to catch the velocity. He hit the floor and from then on it was a crawl on his dreadful knees, all scarred and bruised. A long clamber on hands and knees through the lounge to the kitchen. He pulled himself up, leaning on the lid of the filthy washing machine. Steadied himself as he stood. Then he reached out to grab another bottle. *I doh care.*

He left the kitchen with warm white wine in his hand. He'd uncorked it late last night and forgotten about it. He swayed through the doorway like a pinball and dropped onto the sofa. With the bottle raised to his lips he choked back the dry vinegar, laced with dusty specks.

Halfway through the bottle his head started to clear. His stomach resolved. *Drinkers am good at it, ay we. Drinkers get good at drinking away hangovers.* He pulled a pair of tracksuit bottoms on and his old jumper. Took a bottle of Sherry from the kitchen. Spent ten minutes looking for his keys. Patted his pocket for his pen and notebook – safely zipped away. Went out to the street – Maple Road. It wasn't a bus stop, but the driver always picked him up from the corner.

He slugged on the sherry as he rode the morning bus route – the X96. It ran through the Wrenna into Dudley Town then on to the massive shopping centre, Merry Hill, then Brierley Hill and then the posh end – Stourbridge, Wollaston. After that it came all the way back. He shrugged and tugged at his pockets, rolled cigarettes and choked down the cheap ruddy grog. Anything not to look up. To not look up at the few who ride the X96.

There were those with purple faces like his. There were those with yellow eyelids like his. They all sat holding onto themselves, spluttering. They all sat watching each other with quick, whipping glances. They hurt – they could do damage.

To Dave's right was a wench in fleece pajamas. She didn't stick to the rules. She stared right at him. Nostrils flared.

"The mask knows," she said. "It sees all. All the fragments of mirror on the floor; it sees all. Time ticks on with a mean, stabbing elbow in the ribs. But other masks still watch me."

She glared at Dave with bloodshot eyes. Her arms and legs were folded and she arched forward – her face sticking out and jutting at him. He tried to smile. *But how my face is creased. How my hair is thin. How on my own I am. An old man with crisp eyes focussed on the end.*

"All the masks mock us," she said, jutting her head again. "No one escapes the masks."

He wrestled his pocket for his pen and notebook. Her eyes half-closed in a wrinkled shrink and her spine straightened. She turned away from him.

The bus chugged on around the beat-up streets that frame the Wrenna. Passed the boarded-up stores on Summer Road, piss stained gullies and doorless doorways. Dave slugged his sherry.

He stared at the floor and sucked his teeth as the bus roved along. Listening to the chug-chug, the coughs, the moans and the mutters. And he went around the whole circuit again. He'd lost count. He just went round and round on the bus. He had no plans to advance. No waiting around. He had no need to complete anything. He just went around – again. The bus passed through the palms of housing estates, wriggled through the clammy fingers of high streets, round and over the sinews of the cut ... circulating onwards.

At Merry Hill Shopping Centre, he looked out of the window. A jigsaw, Lego brick mesh. A grey-black web of coiled interzones where thumbs of stainless steel and coloured plains punctured the land. He watched two passengers get on, both in suits. A young man in his twenties and a man much older. Both with the same haircut.

"There's them that do an' them who pass the buck," older guy said as they worked their way up the aisle. "Shifting through the sheets and bouncing the work to the back 'a the queue. And it gets picked up by you. You're the drain cleaner, the fumigator. It's your turn to shine."

"I'm just waitin' on me figures, me settlement," young guy said, sliding on to the seat and shimmying over to make room for his friend.

"There ay a settlement," said old guy. "Just a counting down 'a the clock, and the weeks, and they all fall into each other an' suddenly it's another month gone."

Young guy went quiet. Old guy nodded his head, folded his arms, grinned to himself.

From the top of the Delph, litter bins wart onto the canal bank – pussing scars. Mechanical creatures push and pull at the new builds. The callused flesh of a cycle track and footpath, wrinkles in its asphalt run. The freckled dashing of taverns hidden here and there, the land almost barren. *Everythin"s still from up 'ere, an' a cloud looms over it all.*

At the front of the bus was a man in a long green anorak. The hood was up and hung over his forehead, stopping just above the eyes. He sat facing the swish and drum of the rain at the windscreen. He sat still, shoulders hunched up to his neck, hands in pockets, head slightly bowed. And he coughed with each exhale. And with each cough came a splutter of phlegm and crust. So the window misted with the steam and breath and in its clearing a sticky residue of green, dry mustard remained. *The wheels on the bus go … on and on. Iss my birthdee!*

The X96 lagged through the suburbs, over tiny little ramps, belching around harsh, tight corners – wheezing. Round and round it went. The X96, with the stench of alcohol and tobacco, singed seats and damp upholstery. Electric light thrust through the misty scene with a flicker. A shadow puppet show, of hunched over passengers.

The driver hugged the wheel, leant over it. His fat head pointing out from his fat neck, slowly slanting towards the windscreen. And the wipers whooped and whooshed and flung him back into his seat for a few seconds. And then he tilted himself over the wheel and towards the windscreen again. He snorted as he tipped his pork-body over to the left or the right; twisted his waist and brought the wheel around to steer the machine around the corner.

Dave watched the driver's strange dance, making notes in his book. With his bottle of Sherry clasped between his knees, he hung onto the cold metal of the seat in front as the bus took the turn. Newcomers swayed with the tilt and clatter against the window. He chuckled with a hangover hiss and jump in his seat.

The driver wore a blue uniform that clung to his packed flesh, tearing slightly at the seams, worn and soiled. The fists that gripped the wheel were moist, pale and flabby with large pores and blond hairs. His thick blond eyebrows curled at the ends and pulled the whole of his forehead down in concentration. His lips curled downwards slightly, and his chin tucked up. He was like poached pork and his thick callused skin created large, dog-eared tumours on his face. He leant, he sweated, he jumped and snorted. And at regular intervals the driver brought the bus to a sudden stop and screamed out the destination.

"ighchurch Road, 'olly 'ill."

Some got on. Some got off. Old and new in exchange again, but the ride went on. Dave stayed the distance.

At the back was the hum and jangle of vibrations. A man was lying across the back seats of the bus with his knees raised. In his hands was a clear, glass jar. The jar was full of spider webs. Smokey and thick through the weathered glass. Two small spiders menaced amongst the webs. The man lay on his back with the jar held just above his head – peering up into it through the bottom, watching the bugs through the concave spectrum. He gently breathed onto the bottom of the jar. An orb of condensation built up then dissipated. As he watched the damp cloud evaporate he chuckled to himself – a hic-hic hiss of two short bleats followed by a dry coughing chuckle. The spiders slowly spun threads inside their globe.

Dave sat almost motionless, but for the small shivers and slight rocks, the necessary gulp of sherry from time to time. No one looked away from their own area of seating. No one looked up. No one spoke. Then out of nowhere, the spider-guy jumped up, dropping the jar as he leapt.

"Ahright! Stop the bus!"

He ran down the aisle, shouting as he went.

"Fuckin' ell mate, stop the bus, it's me stop!"

The bus screeched to a halt and the man stretched his legs to jump off in a long quick stride. Then the bus hissed and pulled away.

The tiny jar of spiders rolled back and forth underneath the bus seats with a slow creak and a rising tumble. Dave watched it roll back and forth as he revolved another circle on the X96. He took the notebook and pen from his pocket again and smiled. *My birthdee, ay it.* Reached down to capture the jar as it rolled under his seat and placed it in his lap.

The bus stopped suddenly and the last few passengers got off, deep in the swamps of streets near the hospital. Russell's Hall Hospital, surrounded in electric light and mist – a glaring ray like a UFO within the bleak dusk of its scape. It was dark by now and the moon tried to pierce the smog. The bus driver stepped out and leaned against the street sign. Choked down a peanut butter sandwich and swallowed the smoke of a cigarette, rocking back and forth on his heels. Stretching his crooked spine and flabby chest. All the other passengers ran off – toward the Chinese takeaway, or into their homes along the red brick rows. One man remained hidden inside, behind the seat at the front, swigging on his last dregs of sherry. Ready for another route around.

The bus started up again, this time almost empty. These were the purgatorial hours of the day when the light is a blue haze, when the lampposts start to scream, when there is no one around. He rode the bus alone. The sherry had gone, a hangover had almost begun. Dave closed his eyes to rest. The bus pulled away from the hospital and turned down the barely lit streets of Windmill End Industrial Estate.

The empty bottle of sherry fell from his grip – hit the floor and rolled backwards in a long clatter-roll. He'd tucked his notebook safely away in his pocket. The jar of spiders viced between his thigh and chest as he bowed in sleep. And he slept on. Slept on through the dead roads, the empty estates and locked up works. Slept on through the repeating circular route. Slept on alone.

The bus pulled up at the end of Maple Road. It wasn't really a bus stop. The frost had already appeared. He felt a touch on his shoulder and a slight shake.

"'Ere y'am, Dave. Weem back at yowers now."

He opened one eye and fidgeted. Gave the driver a slight twitch of his lips in an attempt to smile.

"Cheers Sculley, see yo' tomorra."

"Tarra'abit."

He stumbled up Maple Road to his front door. Struggled with the yale lock for a minute, fell inside.

———————

When I visited Alvan's mom she told me she'd found pages of stories like this in a drawer she'd emptied. I thought about all the stories and half-stories *I'd* hidden away. Dave'd delicately folded his in half and placed them in a little writing bureau he'd bought from the Heart Foundation when he'd turned forty. Daily notes. Bits of poems. This one joined twenty-eight years of other daily scraps that'd lain unread, until Dave died and Alvan's mom had found them.

Poplar Crescent

I heard a sound – an unreal sound – a feedback boom. I heard it zip through my head. I still hear it sometimes.

Nick lived up Poplar Crescent. Poplar Crescent wasn't a crescent – it just joined Laurel to Limes. It was basically a straight line. The same flat-fronted red brick semis ran along each side – lawns trimmed to perfection sitting next to rotten fence panels and litter, sitting in turn by posh paved drives and weed-funk.

It was just after Lee Benton's first pissing event in Top Church. I'd laughed so hard my jaw ached and my stomach burned all the way back to the Wrenna.

"Imagine the vicar's face!" Lee said.

I hadn't known Lee that long, and I knew I shouldn't get to know him too well.

"He'll finish at the back by the font," he said. "And he'll walk through the church, and he'll probably be thinking how nice it was to see two boys finding Jesus and then he'll pass the pew where we were."

Lee sat by Nick in Sociology. We didn't even know what sociology was when we took our options. I'd have liked it, I reckon. They got talking about music and films and the usual and they started talking about how there were no proper rock stars anymore. Lee lent Nick his copy of Marilyn Manson's biography.

"The last great rock star," Lee said, and that led them to thinking about the politics of breaking rules. I went along for the ride.

We met outside college and walked back to Nick's. Nick had skived the morning and went to see Burroughs' brother at the basketball courts. Spent a tenner each on a spliff and a bag of shrooms.

"Alright?" Nick had said.

"Who'm yo'?" Big Burroughs said.

"I went to school with yo' brother."

"My brother. Prick, ay 'e?"

"Day know 'im that well."

Big Burroughs looked down at him from his perch on the top of the bench. Squinted.

"It was yower mate who gid 'im a kickin' wor it?"

"Dunno," Nick had shrugged, shook his head, said he'd become very aware of hands, breath, eye contact.

Big Burroughs leaned forward – elbows on knees – leered, scratched his chin and took a long toke of his fag.

"Fair play," he finally released with a cloud of smoke. "'E ay no brother 'a mine now anyroad. Prick ay 'e."

The last I heard of Burroughs he was second choice keeper for Stourbridge Town. He'd done trials at Villa but had a shoulder problem. He did well for Port Vale and Walsall for a little while. Moved off the Wrenna.

Forgot about us and his brother and his dad. Nick told us that Big Burroughs had told him stuff.

"I was always the yampy one in our family," he'd said. "The youngun was dad's favorite. 'E got the new Wolves kit every year, got the new Adidas Predators and everythin'. I got fuckin' hi-tech an' two-stripe tracksuits. He wor never gonna be Peter Schmeichel an' I told him years ago. They stuck me in the cells for meltin' down 'is trophies and scrappin' 'em. An' Dad sent me to live with Mom. With Mom, in fucking Sedgley. Then 'er dies. Then I'm back with the old mon who meks me pay rent. I'm glad the fucker got a kickin'. After 'e left for Port Vale an' 'e stopped coming back, I went to see Dad. Dad told me to go fuck myself. I'm glad the fucker got a kickin'."

I remember, years later, Big Burroughs 'd been inside again and we all went for a drink at the Caves and he was the first one to warn us about the gangs in prison and how they looked like the gangs out here. He'd been released along with a few others and they talked the whole night about the gangs.

"Them tekkin' over," Big Burroughs said. "They doh even want a draw, they want theya law an' theya law only."

We day really take it seriously. We'd watched that new bloke from the council on the Central News and how he'd said his new law had meant that those people who'd been sold out by society and missed out on so much were now getting proper justice. For many of us that made sense. But the gangs had friends and

103

brothers who'd settled at The Caves, and so bit by bit a few more followed along. Then girls started to go missing. And years later, when I'd moved back, I started collecting the bits of newspaper articles I'd seen, and I hid them under my bed with my Navy stuff and my blades.

We got back to Nick's in no time. Big Burrough's 'd rolled a joint for us and told Nick it was a free trial. Nick had brewed a tea.

"Big Burroughs told me iss best to mek a tay," he said. "Gess in the system quicker. Says just cook 'em up in boilin' water for a bit."

He handed us a mug as we went in.

"Tastes like shit," I said. It tasted rotten and metallic and pissy. Cold copper absorbed in muck of grasslands. Earthy. Makes you spit. Green Pool and tadpoles.

"Get it down," Lee said and swigged his back. Lee was two years older than us. He'd dropped out of King Edward's and started again at Dudley College. Nick really liked him. I gulped the tea down.

We sat staring at the walls for about half an hour. Nick had put Massive Attack on the stereo. Lee sparked the spliff up and we passed it about. We sat staring at the walls. Silent.

And I felt a little warmth brew in my stomach and some pulsing in my head and my neck felt tight and heavy but it felt good to rock my head back and forth. *Is this it? Is this coming up? I doh wanna speak fust. I doh wanna be fust.* Then it came. I heard a sound – an unreal sound – a feedback boom I heard zip through my head. A sort of wave up my spine and into my head and it bounced and made my vision dizzy and then it released and it felt like something burst – a beautiful burst that sprinkled through my body. It fizzed and I was overwhelmed. I smiled. It felt like the calming of breath after a cross-country run. Like shitting and pissing when you've had to hold it in. Like that time with Juno Hutton when she ground her pelvis against me. And I thought about Custer and Sitting Bull and I thought about the Shaolin Monks.

"My hand feels like a sponge," Lee said.

"I'm the sofa," Nick said.

We looked at each other for a second. Recognised. Recognised *it*. And fell about laughing.

I was the first to come around. I left Nick and Lee upstairs. Nick said there was nothing to say. We saw a bit less of Lee after that. I slept for a whole day after it. I wondered about things I never wondered about. *How will you be different now?*

I heard a sound – an unreal sound – a feedback boom I heard zip through my head. At first it was just a colour. A glow. Then it grew. It sprouted like splitting cells and spun around. And it grew. More colour. Neon, fluorescent. Spinning. And it grew, sprouted, split cells. It spun around. It grew until all I could see was this constantly moving, splitting cell, spinning of helixes and colours that drew me in. I leaned into it. I fell in. I don't know. I got sucked in.

Then blackness.

Then a tiny white light. It grew. Sprouted like splitting cells. Glowed. And Olwen came from it. Stood before me – pale, thin, wide-eyed, smiling. Something moved behind her – shadows. A figure. I heard a sound – an unreal sound – a feedback boom I heard zip through my head. Two dark arms with huge hands came from behind her. Each hand placed on her front. And it spoke. *There is something coming. War and waste. Every joy is ended in this way. But it can rebuild. And you must rebuild if you want my Olwen.* She looked calm throughout this. Smiling, wide-eyed. Then the hands withdrew. Then the shadow skulked away. Then I slipped back.

The music was finished and I was alone in Nick's front room. Nothing felt right. There were noises coming from upstairs. Creaking rhythms and sighs. *Are you just gonna sit theya? Are you just gonna do what you always do? Just gonna wait. Just gonna be a bit part. Just gonna watch it happen.* I'd turned on myself and felt cold and that rush and release had gone and I didn't want to stand up – I knew I'd catch myself in the mirror. And I thought about how I might not be the same again. Olwen, what girl is this? *You always do this. You're always the onlooker. Call yourself a man.*

Heartbeat was slow. Breath was slow. It was cold. On edge. And I stared at the wall but I was looking in on myself and I thought about Dad and Custer and Juno and the flowers and Olwen laying out by the woods, and I thought I wouldn't be the same again. Dread. I turned on myself. Something was coming. Dread. *There is something coming. War and waste.* I felt it – dread – something waiting to pounce. I stared at the palms of my hands. *Big hands. You've got massive hands. Call yourself a man. Onlooking all the time. Watcher.*

I never took shrooms again. Dabbled with the skunk from time to time.

The first night I spent on base in Portsmouth I was lying in my bunk and I thought about all of this. The dread. The redness. The twinge and the oddness. Smiled. Then shivered. I heard a sound – an unreal sound – a feedback boom I heard zip through my head. And thought about the dread again when I properly moved back. And I thought about it that night up on the reservoir with stares, blood, a hessian sack.

Wren's Nest Road

There was a sort of meadow on the Wrenna, just before you entered the woods. When I'd come back from the Navy I used take a few tins of beer down in the summer, sit and read the paper, the Dudley News. We were close to the end of the local papers then. We weren't to know. I was trying to think and trying to get into the heads of the people who'd done these things and as I read it was like they spoke and I saw their thoughts, like I had done with those pictures of Little Phil when I was a kid.

———————

He lived on Wren's Nest Road, in the new builds. He met her at work. He was broken the moment their eyes met. They began to take walks in the late summer through the park, past the priory ruins, through the woods behind the castle.

He spoke to her and danced with her and walked beside her like a lover. She'd never noticed the white circle of un-weathered skin on his left ring finger, where he'd removed his wedding band each time they met.

After a few months of them seeing each other, he decided to tell her. He prayed she'd understand. He planned to meet her in the park on a late summer evening, they'd walk through the trees and he'd confess. He thought then, they could really be with each other.

He left his house and walked through the estate. Through the winding, narrow streets. And this is where I sat, crouched in the corner of the covet, waiting for him. I watched him stroll past. I counted to three. Then I jumped out with my axe and stuck it deep into his shoulder. He made no noise, falling instantly to the floor.

I made sure he never got round to confessing to his lover, but she definitely found out at the funeral.

———————

The park guy was one of the first to be reported in the newspaper. This was one of the first gang related stories. I was trying to get into their heads – into the thoughts of the victims and the gangs. It made my gut feel empty. I thought about Custer and Sitting Bull and I thought about the Shaolin Monks. *Better a warrior in a garden than a gardener in a war.* That's what Dad had tattooed across his chest. I think the Dudley News had about two more weeks until it croaked.

The Caves

"I nodded at the lads as I walked in," Mark said. "The allotment was done for the day."

The Caves pub was full. Big Burroughs had just got out and his dad had put a buffet on.

"I tried to smile," Mark said. "I doh wanna be that mon anymore. I wanna be a lamb."

"A lamb?" I asked him.

"Like the great JC," he said stuffing pork pie into his gob. "I remember a story me dad used to tell me about a Saxon king who got exiled to Kamber, an' 'e had a lamb, an' 'e'd stroke the lamb's back an' 'e'd feed it an' all that. One day the lamb chewed through a Hemlock bush an' never woke up again."

"Am yo' okay, Mark?"

"I killed an 'oss today," he said. "It was maimed. So I killed an 'oss today."

I got him a pint and we went out for a smoke.

"I've never done wrong," he said. "I just never did anything. I'll kick the shit out 'a myself again."

Bishop Milner Catholic School

"Giz yo' fuckin' money, yo' paki bastard."

They had him pinned against the sports hall wall. Three of them. Burroughs, prick he was, and two others. Burroughs had him by the scruff and was pressing his chest into the bricks. He was the new boy. He'd started just after Christmas. Me and Nick had been mates since primary school and even though there were black kids and Asians and all sorts, the new boy was different. He was skinny and he smelled odd and his uniform was all over the place – blazer too big and trousers too short and he wore those black pumps you used to have for PE. He was a bit dirty and he looked like he'd sid stuff – ghosts or summat.

The first few weeks of January, Burroughs and his mates grabbed the new boy and robbed him and sometimes they took a couple of cheap shots too. Me and Nick were still finding our feet and everyone said Burroughs was hard. I think *he* said it, and it stuck. No one bothered to challenge it and he wore it.

This day at the sports hall was different. Me and Nick were just coming out from football trials. I'd got on the end of one of his long passes that no one had seen coming, but we'd practiced it over and over with his dad. Nick was just outside the area and I started skipping down the left flank. He sent it up and over, weightless, curling, and it looked like it was going to run the whole length of the pitch, then it dropped and I was cutting into the box and it landed at my feet. Nick's dad had shown me how to tap the ball and take the pace out of it. I did. It ran forwards slightly, spinning. Then I hit it. Bottom corner. We still lost but it was a fucking good goal.

"Am yo' deaf, Taliban?" Burroughs asked.

"Yo' son of a cum eating whore," the new boy replied.

Me and Nick pissed ourselves. Full on, no holds barred, belly laugh. Burroughs kicked the lad's feet away and turned to us.

"What the fuck am yo' laughin' at, Ant and Dec?" Burroughs started walking towards us.

"Ha! Ant and Dec. Ant and Dec!" his two muckers started chanting.

We were scared. Burroughs was the hardest in the year and if he day get us his brother would. Big Burroughs was proper hard and he had the broken teeth to prove it. But we were kids and if you hear the words son-of-a-cum-eater come out of the mouth of a lad who didn't sound like us anyway – shit – we couldn't stop laughing.

"Ant and Dec! Ant and Dec!"

"Yo' ay still laughin'," Burroughs said, coming closer.

We had our backs to the sports hall too. The only

112

way out was through him. Then the new boy started up again.

"I fuck your horny mother," the new boy shouted from the floor. "My balls hit your face!"

Burroughs turned and we had two seconds. Nick took his football boots from his bag and wrapped them across the back of Burroughs' head. Studs clattered against skull and Burroughs hit the deck. We legged it.

"Come on, Alvan," Nick called. "Get up."

And he did. Alvan followed us as we legged it. We were all laughing and it took us the rest of lunch time to stop. Me, Nick and Alvan were a proper team from then.

Hazel Road

Snow had cancelled school. Or was it already the holidays? The delicate flakes of icy white come and go. It falls like static blowing in the breezes, sticks to gateposts and hedges, then melts away. Time and snow – perpetually coming and going.

Mom made us take soup over to Auntie Carlin when it snowed.

She told me, "put a teaspoon under yower pillow, bab. Meks it snow."

Olwen giggled and looked right through me, "He doesn't believe you, Bernadette," she said to Auntie Carlin.

She looked like she was made of snow, Olwen did. She was helping Auntie Carlin with a knitted blanket. Each square a slightly different set of triangles and stars. Each square a slight variation in colour.

———————

Our gloveless fingers, encased in frost, burned like they'd swallowed the fire of winter – coming around again.

Winter is coming around again.

"Ya not going out without ya scarf," Mom howled. I heard her, but I'd already slammed the front door. Me, Nick and Alvan ran off through the Wrenna.

Nick said, "less gu offroadin' on the sledges, out in the woods, up on the cliffs."

"My mom says to stay off the cliffs," Alvan said. "She says they put fences up for a reason."

"Fuck yower mom," Nick said. "Less gu offroadin'."

So we did. We had to jump the wire fence they'd put up around the base of the cliffs. We didn't even look to see if anyone was watching. We found the steepest parts of the limestone cliffs and weaved our way up through the trees and ditches. Sat on thin red plastic at the top. You could feel the cold through the bottom of the sledge. Heads up through the canopy, we looked down on the snow-covered roofs on the estate. We were up a height. It was freezing. I got a shiver in my thigh, a little twitch-shiver that worked its way up and around my hips and up and into my arms and down to my feet. I was twitching and I got that feeling like when Dad goes over the bumps in the road too fast. And I got that feeling like when we have to leave for holiday really early, and there's no time for breakfast. A little sleepy. A little wired. A little empty. An oddness. A twinge.

"Wass up with yo'?" Nick asked.

"Just cold," I said.

"The mountains of Wren's Nest," Alvan said.

"Yo saft prick," Nick said and gave him a shove.

Alvan's dive lasted about three seconds. A scream, a flash of falling, a thud. The thud was odd, that thud – it was flat and dull but it stopped everything. It resounded. A low thump pulsed through the Wrenna and went through me. The twitch stopped. I didn't expect cracks and smashes and screams but that thud, that thump!

Alvan lay still at the bottom. Still and silent. The twitch stopped. I broke off. I stuck my heels into the ground and pulled my knees back to launch myself. I can't remember. It was done in a moment. My guts went up and into my throat and my heartbeat thrashed – a thrill of falling for a second or two – then I dug my heels into the icy earth and skidded to a stop.

Alvan was still. Face down. I tiptoed over to him. The twitch was done with but I couldn't breathe. Alvan was stone still. I moved forward in a half-rush, half-tiptoe. Alvan lay where he'd landed, limbs splayed, face down – still. I reached out and stopped myself reaching; went to touch and stopped myself touching. Held my breath. Then I part-scampered over to him. Bent down.

"'Ad ya!" Alvan jumped up with a big grin on his face.

"Yo' cunt!" I said. Exhaled. I felt three beats from my heart. I remember those three kick-start beats. "We thought we'd killed yo'."

"Yo' saft prick," called Nick from high up and launched himself off the top. Again, three seconds. Again, a scream. Again, a flash of falling. Then the thud. And he got Alvan in the leg and sent him flying and he got me in the chest and knocked me back and we all had no breath in us and we all had twitches, we were all soaked and the moms were right – about scarfs and fences.

The wind catches, in its coming and going, outside. It burns and melts. Their cold limbs are infested with joy as the kids are called in – home time always comes around again.

"Gu up town an' walk yower nan 'ome," Mom said. So I did. Nan had gone out for the morning deals on the market. She was convinced the fruit was better before lunchtime.

"They sell the shit stuff to the lunch trade," she said.

She'd gone out and the snow had hit in the two hours between. I ran up Wren's Nest Road, *dunno why I've gotta get 'er it ay even snowin' that bad*, then cut through Meadow road, *alright a little bit slippy on the hills, like, onto Linden, sheet white – not a spare patch of uncovered ground*, and down to Hazel – *inches, within hours: thick packed, crystal snow.*

Hazel Road was a bit posher. They had driveways and big front gardens. Bay windows and all that. It was the edge of the Wrenna but they were alright down there. Most of them were old folks who'd saved their money all their lives.

And it was here I went. I was looking up at the trees and the houses and thinking about the snow but I was being careful – knee-bent, toes pointed out, arms outstretched. I took one step off the curb, my heel went back and I went down. Thud. That thud.

My head hit the pavement. I felt dizzy, sick. Watery mouth. Vision went into, and out from, a slight tunnel. I heard a sound – an unreal sound – that feedback boom I heard zip through my head. Then the long ping of ringing ears. I blinked and the sky was pearl. I blinked and it rolled. I blinked and saw three faces looking down over me. Left – Auntie Carlin. Right – The Laurel Witch. Top – Olwen. They smiled and they said something and I couldn't hear but I saw Auntie Carlin shake her head and I saw the Laurel Witch shrug and laugh and Olwen looked a little teary. And I turned my head to watch them walk off and the two elders led Olwen down towards the woods. Olwen turned before the end of the road. Looked back at me.

"Ay it yo' who ought to be rescuin' me?" Nan stood behind me grinning. Held out a hand to help me up.

"Did you see Olwen and . . . " I started.

"Ay no one out in this, bab," she said.

She helped me up and we worked our way back up to hers.

And now, as they sting and burn; that is what's most noticeable – numb fingers after the snow.

Cedar Road

They were on their own. The allotments were barren, they always were these days. He still whispered as he spoke. Everything needed to be careful now. They'd cut through the caves on the Wrenna to get through. The gangs hadn't realised what lay in there. The gangs were running things now.

They took a seat on the bench they'd made together from scrappin' the plots that no one came to anymore. Mark had etched Jackie's name into the wood. They were the last two growers on this patch. They still did well despite the soil. Kyle sparked a roll-up, passed it to Mark then did the same for himself.

"Beans am lookin' alright." Kyle said.

"They am ar. An' the pays." Mark replied.

"Ar."

"Nothin' but dandelions on the rest 'a 'em now."

"Shame ay it? Jackie'd 'ave 'ad 'eart attack."

"'Er would've, ar. I'd rather 'ave sid 'er gu that way than under their 'onds though."

"Too right. Cunts."

"That little Phil," he spat. "Cunt!" Mark spat on the ground.

The allotments were barren. Just Mark and Kyle left. Covered in weeds, ruins of sheds and greenhouses, rusted troughs, rotten fences and scorched out earth. The land sits between the criss-cross streets of the estate, the woods and the park. There used to be old railway tracks there. The tracks were laced with foxgloves and goosegrass these days. No one went into Brum anymore, not that way anyway. Most of the estate was boarded up: the pub; the community centre; the rows and rows of terraces. Mark and Kyle had been stubborn with their homes. They still lived next door to each other on Cedar Road. Mark had taken a sledgehammer to the kitchen wall to connect the homes. He'd put the head of one of the gangs through it first when *they'd* tried to clear them out. Kyle put the body in the woodchipper.

"'Ere's some fertiliser for yo' Jackie," Kyle laughed as he spread the bits of guts and bone over the allotment.

———————

Eventually they knocked down The Caves pub and built a funny tall building – skinny, glass and bland-looking. We called it the temple. A huge car park surrounds it. A guy comes and shouts out from the top on a small balcony five times a day. A cat's cry, five times a day. That was alright for us. A bunch of Skinheads who knew Big Burroughs came down a few times, making a big deal about it all and starting fights. We knew Alvan

120

and his mom though, and by then his cousins were all on the Wrenna too, and most of them had married and had kids and some were brown and some were little milk-coffee sorts.

Jackie always said, "If yo' get yower round in, yo' doh grass an yo ay a cunt yo'm alright."

Thass how we all were.

The Skinheads had come down to protest and cause trouble and we'd got in on the fight against them. *I've lived next door to Farooq for three years, Christ we break fast with 'em sometimes, Christ 'e picks me kids up from school.* We all felt like that, so we rallied together against the Skins. Nick had his nose broke and I got a suspended sentence for looking after Alvan and his mom. The skins day make any difference out between the gangs and anyone else who was different.

And eventually there was this new bloke on the council who'd rushed through a new law that saw about a hundred cons released from Oakwood and Brinsford and then loads of them came down the Wrenna when they were bailed. A few at first. Then more. And they moved into where The Caves pub used to be. That was the proper start of the gangs. And they were just like Big Burroughs had said they were. And the Skinheads came again. This time we all formed a human chain around the building that used to be The Caves pub. We kept the Skins at bay. And we chanted *Every Daughter, Every Son, The Wrenna's 'ere for Everyone.*

And these ex-prisoners moved in to where The

Caves pub was and they started talking about banning smoking and closing the other pubs and making the girls and boys go to different schools. Some of our lot thought it was just noise. Some of our lot thought it might be good to have new ideas and things, and some of our lot joined the gangs. Some of our lot just turned a blind eye to it all. Kept schtum. Kept out of immediate harm.

You'd see groups of these gangs, these ex-cons patrolling the streets. That little Phil, hiding behind a pack of them.

The Skinheads came down a third time and the police kept them at a distance, up the top end of Cedar Road. Most of us stopped at home this time.

Girls started going missing. Some of the girls on the estate. Mrs Maleh had had her head kicked in the week before. Polish Pete got sent down for three years for defending Juno after the gangs caught her drunk one night in a skin-tight dress.

Folks started moving out of the estate. Little by little. Year by year. The gangs started buying the homes up. Little by little. Year by year. Girls started going missing. Our old primary school was now a centre for mothers and girls and our old Catholic school became a boys' school. The kids stopped playing on the Wrenna. No one went out at night. And eventually Jackie tried to set fire to the place with some cedar wood – the Laurell Witch'd told her "we use it in the garden to ward off moths."

I thought about all of this, that night up at the

reservoir. The water. The blood. That boy's Machete from that night in Helmand. And I thought about Sitting Bull. And I thought about Dad.

———————

Mark and Kyle stayed away from the gangs and they stayed away from the skinheads. They stayed clear of the police. But they never moved. They barricaded themselves in. They worked through the limestone caves on the Wrenna. They kept tending their plot.

They spread her ashes on the allotments. Mark and Kyle were the last two growers – in the plot that backs on to the park and the woods. Jackie was Mark's wench.

"Better gerr'off, ay we, Mark."

"Ar, we'll only 'ave an hour now until iss dark."

Kyle took a hip flask from his jacket, took a swig and passed it to Mark. Mark did the same then splashed some onto the ground.

"See yo' tomorrow, Jackie."

Dudley Chronicle

Tributes to Dudley Woman, who died following recent protests.

TRIBUTES have been paid to the woman who died after being trampled in Dudley protests yesterday who has been named locally as Jackie Gabbard. Community leaders around the borough have been posting their condolences and prayers for the 59-year-old who died of her injuries yesterday afternoon. She had been taken to hospital after the recent protests connected with the so-called Berresford Law, which has seen dozens of ex-prisoners move into the local area. Police confirmed this morning that she did not survive and they have now launched a murder investigation.

Community leader Dr Kaur confirmed the tragic news on Facebook, saying: "With unbelievable sadness I'm having to inform you of the passing away of Jackie Gabbard. This woman was loved by all, once you met her you never forgot her, she was guaranteed to make you smile."

Dudley Canal and Tunnel Trust, whom Jackie volunteered with, also announced the sad news on its Facebook page, saying: "We extend our deepest condolences to the family."

Councillor Berresford added, "Whilst I'm deeply saddened to hear the news of Ms Gabbard's untimely death, I want to reiterate just how much hurt has been felt by these illegal protest movements against a group of society who have been unfairly maligned for too long. I hope this tragedy helps to reshape the narrative for Dudley and the Wren's Nest going forward."

Police say specialist officers have been supporting the family and they have been working round the clock to try to find who was responsible for the killing and why it happened.

Spinney

You could never get too deep into the woods. Our estate wrapped around it. But there were hard to reach paths and hard to find parts. We'd play wargames when we were kids. You never forget the changes in smells when the seasons slowly shifted. Sometimes you'd see a small pile of beige limestone. Like a burial mound. I'm not sure how well we remember these things. Sometimes you'd see movements and sometimes you'd hear footsteps, and you could never be sure if it was Auntie Carlin or Olwen or the Laurel Witch. And sometimes you were sure it was none of them. And you'd quietly back away.

Ash Road

He smoked a pipe: its black skin is matt and dented from bite marks and scars where he tasted and emptied ashes. It invites you with a curve: a resting knee beneath a table.

The house smells of charred old books.

He smoked a pipe: it sits on the arm of an old yellow chair, stained with wine and whiskey, spilled over years. Sitting – waiting for its owner to taste its hollow arm.

Old books and all-day stews trace the musky room. Old Ernie limps and chews on pickled eggs. He is thrifty, he tunes the radio to Holst, watches others play Chinese whispers, shrugs, tuts, looks out at the garden he can longer tend, having only one good leg. He lost his knee fighting the MNLA in the Malayan jungle.

The limb of the pipe is brought up to his lips. With each pout and suck it steams. Deliberate inhales. Slow. Deliberate exhales. Slow.

This is the pipe, that's all. All that remains on Ash Road. One Boxing Day his heart gave in. Ernie was Dad's Dad. I was too young to know him.

Ivy Road

I am a torpedo. I am a torpedo. I am a torpedo. His morning mantra accompanied every early swim, every stretch and pull of his limbs through the water. *I am a torpedo.* This chant matched the rhythm of each stroke, each length, over and over again. Each morning. *I am a torpedo.* A ritual, every day easing out the whisky smear of the night before. Each night alone with his semi-automatic sniff of amphetamine, ingested along with the strict stopwatch hourly tick-tock of a cuckoo clock. Cuckoo! Cuckoo! She'd made him a Valentine's gift of it almost a decade ago.

———————

"I love you, James. It was my grandad's. Pretty much every cog and screw's been restored but still, it's about sixty years old. His wife gave it to him before they left Germany. He always kept it on German time."

"Then so shall I. I love it and I love you."

He nailed the clock to his studio wall. They lay wrapped in each other on his tatty, yellow sofa, listening to their breathing, their heartbeats, the churn of the clock and its occasional chirp. The slight mutter of the neighbours; passing traffic. They lay, drifting in and out of sleep. James' folks had died before he'd met Lauren.   The yellow sofa was all he'd inherited. Mustard arabesques were stitched into the wool, now frayed, stained, balding.

———————

"Doh forget yower sister," his dad always told him. "And doh tek anythin' fer yo'self that means another bugger suffers."

"I know, Dad. How many times?"

"As many as it teks, James, before I 'ear a promise I can trust."

"I promise you."

———————

These days he was alone every night with whisky and pistachio nuts – the only nutrients and the only distraction between half hourly snorts of speed. In the early hours he'd scribble notes and tickle piano keys – everything scrapped the next day before the swim. *I am a torpedo. I am a torpedo.* Fingers gripped the edge of the pool and this mantra continued as deep breaths steeped into slow, calm tastes of air. *I am a torpedo. I. am. A. Tor-pe-do.*

Lauren didn't get to see the pool. His mom, dad, and sister didn't either.   He'd moved out to the Cheshire Countryside. Away from the tangles of Ivy

Road. An escort would ask to see it sometimes, but it was James'. He'd played piano back at college, spent every breaktime with Lee Benton. We took the piss back then, but it'd scored big for him. He learned how to tickle ivory and how to never look a gift horse in the mouth.

———————

"An oss ay it?" His sister still lived on Ivy Road. She'd done the house up with Matt, a mechanic from Dixons Green, who always got a round in and charged mate's rates to everyone. Dad said, "There's no one knows more about a werritin' motor an' 'er fixes bostin fittle, 'er could 'ave 'er own cafe, 'er could. 'Er' only 'as to light the lard an' 'er ends up feedin' the street. There ay no one better. They ay got much but what they've got they share, doh they?"

———————

I am a torpedo. I am a torpedo. The mantra followed his swift pull up out of the pool, followed his slow stride around the edge, the slick slide of the patio doors. *I am a torpedo.* He collapsed on to the yellow sofa to sleep the rest of the day. This heirloom was home to hangovers, downers, heartbreak. Simple. Calm. Warm. Face pushed into cushions. He was as trapped as he was secure.

———————

"Come on, James, t'ay nothin'." Mother cradles her oldest son. She spits on a tissue and swabs the graze on his thigh. Slides and circles the wound slowly, tender – saliva-soaked strokes. James' tears dry. Sobs calm.

"Warrappened?"

"I tripped up."

"Racin' our Steph again, was yo'?"

James nods.

"Y'om my lickle torpedo, ay yo'?"

James smiles, coughs a half-laugh. Buries his face into Mother's breasts.

———————

His face was now pushed into the yellow sofa – sinking into its musk of whisky and nicotine, its stains of sex and blood. That's where he stayed most mornings. That or walking in and out of empty rooms. Reading sheet music he wrote five years ago. Conducting as he skims the pages. Walking in and out of empty rooms. He sips coffee. Watches afternoon quiz shows. Walks in and out of empty rooms.

———————

"Which author," Sandy Toksvig asks. "Gives his name to a condition where the sufferer experiences overwhelming and often hysterical responses to . . . "

"Stendhal," Lauren shouts at the TV. "That's another item of clothing, James."

He slips out of his boxer shorts.

"You look like a goose in just your socks."

"Oh, do I?"

"You do."

"Well, I don't know what kind of geese you lot get up here in Cheshire but back in Dudley we've got some real tough bastards."

"Is that a threat?"

"Just a thought."

He jumps up and pins her down. Bites her neck. Moves his hands over her. Rests on her cunt.

"In which South American country do they celebrate the day of the . . . "

"Mexico," Lauren shouts. "You know the rules, James."

James whips off a penultimate sock. Staring into each other's eyes, they kiss, they giggle into each other's mouth. Cuckoo! Cuckoo!

Six thirty was a good time. He'd set it himself. He liked this time. No longer afternoon. Not quite evening. Fine to drink but still feels like a treat. His strict six thirty routine was as close to normal as he got. He was like that at college too. Always a bit here and there, iverin and overin, but then you'd see him at the piano.

"The rest 'a the world might be guin' to shot," his dad spat. "But weem 'ere, 'round the family table fer tay."

Mom blushed, smirked, nodded and they all tucked in.

"'Ow did piano gu today, James?"

"Good."

"Good. Just good? I ay forkin' out fer just good."

"Mr Mansell tode us about the rites 'a spring today 'e did ar," James said; he still had the coal in his lungs back then. "Thass wharr'I'm learnin'."

"The Rytes 'a Spring. Sounds posh."

"Apparently," James said. "When they fust played it, cus it was so new, the audience rioted and torn the theatre up!"

"I doh know about that, son."

"Imagine though, Dad, mekin' summat so out theya that people doh know 'ow to behave an' lose all sense."

"Like yower mom when 'er gess on the karaoke down the Spills."

They all laughed at that. Dad stuck a hunk of chicken in his mouth – chewed and smiled at the same time.

"Spaykin' 'a which," Mom said. "Ay it darts tonight?"

"'Tis ar," Dad said. Turned to James. "'Urry up then, mucker."

"I ay up ferrit tonight, Dad . . . I . . . doh really like it."

His dad said it didn't matter. He looked at Mom as he said it.

"Yo'll be on yower own," his mom said. "Me an' Steph am guin' up Merry 'ill."

"I doh mind, I wanna practice my pieces."

133

"Now," Dad said. "Thass a good idea. Yo've gorra proper skill theya, lad. Like yower grandad an' his runner beans – they doh grow less yo' water em."

Later, as they were leaving, he heard his dad say, "It doh matter," to his mom. He didn't recognise what the tone in his voice was until a few years on.

———————

James rested an almost full bottle of whisky and a half empty tumbler on his piano. Dipped a pinky in a plastic bag of white powder and rubbed it over his gums. Lit a cigarette and started to play. Twenty seconds in, his finger missed a key, and the chord came out sharp. He thunder-clapped the board. Grabbed the whisky and gulped. Took a toke of his cigarette. Fought back the watery-mouth-vomit feeling. Started again. Better this time. Treated himself to a line of meth.

———————

After uni he moved in with Matt and Steph. We all saw a bit more of him then, but he wasn't one for dominoes or drinking and I think he held a grudge from the teasing we gave him at college. I always wanted to ask him about Lee Benton. *Bend over for Benton*, that's what we'd say. Nick and Alvan used to throw sweets at him in the refectory. I wondered if Lee and James had done any pissing together. What had Lee shown James? He must have shown him something. There was something about Lee that marked you, and James had been close to him back in the day. James worked part time at the bookshop up Merry Hill. Got back to his sister's at about three each day.

Steph was twenty-five and had three kids. They'd let themselves into his room and were banging and plonking on the piano. James rushed the door.

"What the fuck is going on here?"

"I'm playin' all the right notes," Steph said. "Just not necessarily in the . . . "

"Get out!" James shouted. "Get the fuck out! This isn't a fucking toy!"

Steph ushered the kids out. Turned and stared at her brother.

"'Ow dare yo'?" she said. "'Ow dare yo' spake like thar'ere, in front 'a yower nieces!"

"How dare you?" James said. "How dare you let yourself into my room and . . . "

"Who's room? Yo' pay any rent, James? Gu an' live with the old mon if yo' ay gorra sense 'a 'umour."

"You know I like things just so, Steph."

"Yo' can suck it up and live 'ere, James, or yo' can gu an' fuck off."

Matt talked her down later and he took James for a pint after tea. He was just like their dad.

It was only a few weeks later that James got a commission to do thirty seconds of music for an advert. Got himself a bedsit in Harborne. Just a bus ride back to family but far enough away to stop daily visits. Two or three commissions came after that. Then more. He got himself a Lexus.

An hour or so at the piano and he'd plodded his way through a few of his favorites. By eight he was back on the sofa. Sipping cigarettes. Sucking up whisky. Snorting more meth. He scribbled down crochets and quavers.

He jumped up. Not Eureka! The bile of his stomach. He spent twenty minutes retching over the toilet. Nothing came up. Just clear phlegm, the odd spots of blood, tissue. Bits of half-digested pistachio. By ten, whisky in hand, he was walking in and out of empty rooms. He spent a while looking at the bathroom mirror.

I am a torpedo! Who is? You? I am a torpedo. You're nothing. Look at you. What did you ever do? I wrote the soundtracks to three award winning films, I scored the theme music to ... what awards? Cannes! Fucking Cannes. It's not the Oscars is it? I've got two Ivor Novellos. You've got shit. Even Cliff Richard got awards. I am a torpedo. I am a torpedo. You're a has-been. You can't think of anything new to do. You fill your time with nothing. You fill your body with shit. You haven't got two notes to rub together. I work. What have you done in the last five years except get royalties? That kids' film with the alien lizards. Come off it! Even children hated that shit. We've farted better art than that. You needed bread and you did it. Don't say it. You sold out. You fucker. I am a fucker and I'm fucking you. Sell out. Fucking talking alien lizards. What have you done in the last five years?

James met Lauren in Cannes. A lucky move with a crazy German director got them a hit.

"A road film," Kinsky said. "I've talked to Volkswagen. A car film, you know. It's going to be fucking great. Like German Easy Rider, but viz cars, viz Volkswagen unt ze beautiful autobahn."

Lauren had a birthmark on the small of her back, the shape of a cat – the silhouette of a cat, sat upright. He was sitting in a cafe whistling to himself.

"Hmmm, Bartok." A voice said.

"Yeah," he answered, turning his face.

"Get you anything else?"

Lauren stood in a pair of shorts, stained by scraps of food. A t-shirt, clinging to skin, sweat soaked. Her short brunette hair tied back with a plait to one side. Ashen neck and shoulders – lean, taut, sculpted. James took it in with a snapshot glance then rested on her dark, umber eyes.

"You know, Bartok?" he asked.

"Well yeah," she turned to walk away. "Even a waitress has ears."

He got up and followed with quick steps.

"E'sprit d'escalier," he said.

"What?"

"When you think of what to say after you've . . . "

"Yeah, I know what it means. What do you mean?"

"I dunno."

"Well?"

"Well what?"

"Well, I've got tables."

James smiled an apology and turned away.

———————

James flicked through the manuscripts, his eyes strained to focus. Unfolded and uncrunched, then tossed them in the air. *Shit! Shit! Shit! Shit! It's all shit! Told you. Some fucking torpedo you are.* Hours' worth of pages of work skidded as they kissed the floor. He returned to the sofa. Returned to the whisky. He stared at the ceiling with tight eyes. The room was a wreck of torn, screwed and scattered manuscripts, overflowing ashtrays, the fungus of old stains. He fingered the pistachios that were now just a bowl of empty shells.

———————

"'Er loved pistachios, thass why them 'ere."

"I know, Dad, but at her ... "

"Don't 'I know Dad' me. Iss 'er funeral and 'er loved pistachios, an' 'er was my wife an' 'er was yower mother, an' there wor no one berra than 'er ... not even yo'!"

Dad squared up to James, prodded a chainmaker's finger into his chest. Looked him dead in the eye.

"Weem proud 'a yer, James. Yower mom was proud as punch. But now ay the time. Not now. T'ay time to play that saft game."

James took a step back. Wiped his face.

"And what 'saft' game is that, Dad?"

His dad took a step towards him. Looked down his chin at him.

"The I play piano, I ate frois gras, I'm a fuckin' faggot, game. Thass what!"

Matt tried to stop James leaving. He knew it was just the grief. James gave Matt a smirk, stepped out the pub for the last time.

"Iss wierta off a duck's back, James," Steph said the next day. She was hungover. She didn't understand the weight of James' goodbye.

After four or five minutes of fingering the bowl, he tossed the empty shells to the floor with the vacuum of stagnant dregs, dry butt-ends and the edits and re-edits of trashy scores.

Mayfield Road

I wander Dudley streets – old canals and factories. All faces are sad now. I take a road I've never been down before.

It has rained. The road is slippery. Time is too late. The slippery road takes time to go down. Alone. Black tarmac and morning shadows. No one has used these sites, where rusted chains mark metal doors, left empty when the change came. Withered parts of machines and machinists beacon the pavements. In the room at the end of the road a curled finger seduced me inside.

A redness comes over me sometimes.

On these streets – the ghost stench lingers.

Linwood Road

Last time I saw Juno she was walking back from the pub. I still had those flowers from the woods. I'd pressed the pink petals in a copy of the Ladybird Book of Custer's Last Stand. You still noticed her all these years on. She was wearing one of those skin-tight dresses with the fluorescent Aztec patterns. It clung to every curve and framed her tight flesh in cello lines. You still noticed her. She was hammered that night. Zig-zag walking. Hiccups. I was heading up the road and she was heading back. We met on the corner of Linwood Road, just where it curves around into the woods, up and over Mon's Hill. I stood aside to let her pass.

"Dirty little shit," she said with a smile. I laughed.

"'Ow do, Juno?" I asked.

"Yo' know very well 'ow I do," she said. She looked me up and down, pursed her lips and her hips rolled slightly as she shimmied past me. There was a slight arch of her back and she pushed her tits out, then straightened again.

141

I smiled at that and it made my head go tight again and I felt hot and cold and sticky handed. And maybe I should follow her and maybe it'd be tender and fierce all over again. A few drops of sweat dripped from my pits and brow. That twitch. That twinge. And I tasted the vodka and the sauerkraut and the itching again.

We looked at each other for a second. She looked me right in the eye. The corners of her mouth curled up. Eyebrow raised. She'd had a life, our Juno, she'd done things. But she always looked tough. And she always looked gorgeous. And, that night, she looked happy too.

"Goodnight, Juno."

"Tarraabit, bab."

Juno said she liked to dance so when we'd both left school I took her out one night. This was between Lee and her getting back with Polish Pete. We went to the cut down by the Black Country Museum. We kissed. It was only once and it was just a kiss. Then we danced a bit and she made me promise not to tell anyone. We held each other and rocked to and fro and she kissed me. I made her promise not to tell too. I still thought of her now and I cried. I'd buy her flowers and I'd throw them in the cut, where we'd danced and kissed.

Osses grazed on the grass down there and in their eyes you could see fear and silence. They were powerful and pathetic.

It's where the carriageway runs up and over the old bridges and ripples the brown water. Commuters pass through every hour of the day and I wonder if they see the eyes of Juno who liked to dance and who kissed me.

Not long after I saw her that last time Juno was in the Dudley News. Face battered and bruised. Lips and nose swelled up. She was bloated by the beating and they told us no one saw a thing. We stopped getting the free paper a week later. That was just before Polish Pete got picked up by the police. He was a big bloke, Pete, and he'd served in the Polish Army, he said it was the Grom or something. Juno had told him about the attack. He'd marched a few of his mates down Linwood Road and met a group of the ex-prisoners who sort of patrolled the streets and the little entrances into the woods. Those gangs. Pete got ten years for gbh, and the judge had taken into account his special army training, so we wouldn't be seeing him for some time.

That was the last time I sid Juno. I still had those flowers from the woods. I'd pressed the pink petals in a copy of the Ladybird Book of Custer's Last Stand.

Rosewood Road

Last time our eyes met your thirst was quenched with syringes.

She could only muster a mouthful every day or two. I tossed seeds on the patch of turf by her window, so her garden birds might distract her tumour. Bedridden where we used to call the living room. Turning, I mouthed *mornin'*. And Mom mouthed it back.

Lilac Road

It was our last summer break. Dudley College A-levels were done. Childhood, almost done. We weren't kids but we still lived with our moms. We were getting ready. We were waiting. We were stalking towards something.

I cut through the woods between Dudley Castle and the Priory Estate. I never normally did that. Those woods were different – you could still hear the traffic on the Tipton Road, you couldn't see anything but trees. It was evening. Just shadow and the faint outline of tipped waste and scrambler tracks.

I hadn't seen her since the Pentecost fete. I'd seen her about but not seen-seen her. She'd come and go like this throughout my life. She'd wraith the Wrenna like this.

It was evening. She still had that creased dress and that matted hair. What girl is this? Olwen.

She was lying in the wide space where the trees and shrubs make way for waves of limestone. Hands folded behind her neck. Nestled in the peaks and troughs of rock. Staring at the stars.

"Them lovely ay they?" I said. Sat down next to her.

"They're dead," she replied. "It's a trick of light. Those stars are already dead. What we're looking at is the light delayed and distorted by time and space. Nothing we see is without delay, without distortion. We can't live outside of space and time but we can't trust it either. It's not what it seems. That's life that is. Light is life. It gives life. It needs space and time to hide in. It needs what delays and distorts to sustain itself."

I nodded. Scrunched my eyes up. I should've clasped my hands together, tapped my finger on my chin or summat. And she was lovely and odd, and it was dark and hard to see and no one would see us if we wanted to do something and was she waiting?

"This light is too far from home to reach us as real – as life giving. All things live and die in time and space. Even the light. We never know if what we're looking at is already gone."

"Profound," I'd heard Nan say it to Father Stephen. "Do you still sing?"

She turned towards me and grabbed my hand. Stole my eyes.

"In some places," she sat up, "The moon appears larger, flowers open their buds to pray for it. The sea seeks the shore more ferociously. Time spins, freezes, expands and melts – leaves cracks in space. Cracks where patterns breed. The sun is slowly burning out of fuel."

She'd stolen my eyes. I couldn't look away.

"A vulture searches out thermals. There are insects in its plumage that no one has ever catalogued, and they feed on a flower that peaks for a moment only, on a cactus, in a small ridge, high above a dry gorge. One small moment of unobserved dance is all it needs. Then it sleeps."

She kissed me on the hand and kissed me on the wrist – the soft inside veiny part of the wrist – and I never sid her again.

Shavers End Reservoir Two

There was a gap in the black wrought iron fence. Likely I'd come through it with a tear of some sort. The blood marked everything I touched. The mist stroked the concrete and steel of the reservoir's bulwark. I stepped up, tip tapping soles against metal steps. I stared at the dark waters. I stared at the blood. Stared like I'd done every time I'd been caught, almost been caught, wanted to be caught. I stared at the hessian sack. I was caught in the stare. Mist. Water. Stillness. I opened the sack.

If I apologise an' 'fess up like them want me to then I'm done, ay I. I wo' say it. I cor. Them gangs am gonna want me to mek amends, pay fer it. Them gangs am gonna want absolution or abolishment. Mom'd say, mek em wait an' they wo' do nothin', mek 'em wait an' remember what yower old mon tode yo'.

I opened the sack and shook out the contents into the waters. The flimsy flesh of the ten scalps I'd taken, dropped into the dank reservoir that used to feed our homes.

The Ley

The Wren's Nest – part housing estate, part nature reserve – the Wrenna, we call it.

Here's where the Dudley Bug was torn from the earth. Where rodents, birds and sneaky mammals lurk. Where caverns and bell pits sit strong in limestone frames. Where trees nestle with grasses and nettles. Where Green Pool sits and sends out its rare stench. It seems still. It is still here. A litter of foxes learn to avoid the traffic. Hawthorns learn new ways to grow thorns. Prehistoric waves mark out our veins. This is not a metonym, it is where we live. The boarded up and barren houses are not symbols. They still orbit the woods. There are only a few of us left. A brook remains from the pluera streets, but a brook still has its current. We await rains. We look still. We are here still. We are the frog spawn that slicks in silica sheets – somehow breeding.

You say you don't walk through here at night. You say to be careful, avoid us. But we are here. Fewer in number, almost motionless. Almost quiet.

We're Wrenna, ay we?

Acknowledgements

Thanks to the editors of Obliterati Press, Burning House Press, Three Drops Press, The Black Country Arts Foundry, Eunoia Review, Flash Fiction Magazine and Anti-Heroin Chic where early versions of some of these pieces were first published.

About the Author

R. M. Francis is a lecturer in Creative and Professional Writing at the University of Wolverhampton. He's the author of five poetry pamphlets.

His debut novel, Bella, was published with Wild Pressed Books and his collection of poems, Subsidence, is out with Smokestack Books.

Printed in Great Britain
by Amazon